"WHAT IS UP, MAD BEA[...]

IT'S BEEN A WHILE! I'D LOVE T[...] THE MADHATTEY COMMUNITY, [...] SUPPORT. I'M TRULY GRATEFUL FOR YOUR LOVE FOR MY STORIES. YOUR ADMIRATION INSPIRES ME TO KEEP PUSHING MYSELF TO DO WHAT I LOVE, EVEN THROUGH MY DARKEST TIMES. THANK YOU SO MUCH MADDIES, MY GREATEST FRIENDS, AND MY UNCONDITIONALLY LOVING FAMILY! ♥

INCLUDING MY MOM, WHO IS ONE OF MY BESTEST FRIENDS IN THE WHOLE WORLD."

WARNING: STORY WILL CONTAIN SERIOUS ISSUES, SUCH AS HOMOPHOBIA, PTSD, AUTISM DISCRIMINATION, ETC. READ AT OWN RISK.

HONORABLE MENTIONS:
KELLY (BEST GAL)
MARZSIE (BEST BRUH)
THANK YOU FOR TELLING THIS STORY WITH ME!! ♥

CREATORS OF BE MORE CHILL:

NOVEL BY NED VIZZINI
PLAYWRIGHT BY JOE TRACZ
MUSIC BY JOE INCONIS
PRODUCTION BY STEPHEN BRACKETT

CREATORS OF DEAR EVAN HANSEN:

PLAYWRIGHT AND BOOK BY STEVEN LEVENSON
MUSIC BY JUSTIN PAUL
BENJ PASEK
PRODUCTION BY MARC PLATT
ADAM SIEGAL

HOW 'BE MORE SINCERE' WAS BORN:

WAVING THROUGH A WIINDOW!

MICHAEL IN THE BATHROOM!!

IN EARLY 2018, TWO AWESOME FRIENDS INTRODUCED BOTH MUSICALS TO ME, 'DEAR EVAN HANSEN' AND 'BE MORE CHILL'. IT BROUGHT BACK A LOT OF MY LOVE FOR MUSICAL THEATER! BOTH STORIES WERE BASED ON NOVELS; HEARTWARMING, HILARIOUS, RELATABLE AND COMPELLING MORALS!

THESE MUSICALS AND THEIR AMAZING CAST ALBUMS WERE WHAT INSPIRED ME TO CROSSOVER THEIR STORIES, AKA 'BE MORE SINCERE'.

[BOTH CAST ALBUMS AVAILABLE ON SPOTIFY/ITUNES ♥]

JARED KLEINMAN (PLAYED BY WILL ROLAND) IMMEDIATELY BECAME MY FAVORITE CHARACTER CAUSE OF HIS DARK SENSE OF HUMOR HEH! MICHAEL MELL (PLAYED BY GEORGE SALAZAR) ALSO BECAME A QUICK FAVORITE FOR HIS JOYFUL PERSONALITY. BECAUSE OPPOSITES ATTRACT, KELLY (MY AWESOME FRAND) AND I THOUGHT THEY'D HAVE AN INTERESTING RELATIONSHIP! ♥ THIS IS HOW THE MUSICAL CROSSOVER STARTED.

JARED, CYNICAL SARCASTIC BEAN. (DEAR EVAN HANSEN)

MICHAEL, GIDDY WEED BABY. (BE MORE CHILL)

MELLMAN ♥

TIMOTHY KLEINMAN, CHEZ BOY! INSPIRED FROM "I'M COOL" LYRICS BY SAM SALMOND.

BENJAMIN KLEINMAN, CHUB BOY! INSPIRED FROM "ONE THING YOU SHOULD KNOW." LYRICS BY BRAVERMAN AND HASSLER.

WILL ROLAND'S ACTING HAS ALWAYS BLOWN ME AWAY! EXTREMELY FUNNY AND WITTY, LIKE EVERYONE'S CRAZY UNCLE. I'VE WATCHED ALMOST EVERY PERFORMANCES ON YOUTUBE, EVEN MADE MY FIRST ANIMATIC "CIGARETTE" LYRICS BY SAM SALMOND.

TWO SPECIFIC SONGS FIRED IDEAS IN MY HEAD, I CAN'T HELP BUT CREATE TWO BROTHERS FOR JARED, HENCE THE KLEINMAN BROTHERS WERE BORN! I'VE SAID IT MANY TIMES, BUT THIS CROSSOVER STORY WOULDN'T HAVE EXISTED IF IT WEREN'T FOR WILL ROLAND, DEH AND BMC.

THIS IS A SHORTENED SUMMARY! MORE INFO HERE: THEKLEINMANBROTHERS.WORDPRESS.COM

BIRTHDAY: MARCH 28, 2002

- 17 YRS OLD.
- HIGH SCHOOL SENIOR
- AUTISTIC

BIRTHDAY: MARCH 16, 1983

- 36 YRS OLD
- LAWYER
- BEST DAD/BRO.

THE KLEINMAN BROTHERS!!

CHANGES:

ALL BROTHERS USED TO LOOK THE SAME (WILL ROLAND), BUT THIS YEAR I DECIDED TO REDESIGN BENJI AND JARED TO HOPEFULLY LESSEN CONFUSION IN FUTURE COMICS! I CHOSE CAMERON J BOND AS INSPIRATION CAUSE HE MAKES BENJI LOOK MORE DAD; MEANWHILE, SKY LAKOTA-LYNCH PORTRAYED JARED IN THE MUSICAL 'DEAR EVAN HANSEN' WHICH I HEARD, HE'S TRULY MADE FOR THE ROLE!

FABULOUS!

PRIDE!!

2018

2019

7

ANDIE KLEINMAN AKA. BEST MOM!
M-MAMA!
NOW AREN'T YOU A CUTE 'LIL BUNNY?
HEY THERE! JARED, RIGHT?
ON MY WAY HOME, I GOT YOU CONDOMS, JUST IN CASE.
...M-MOM, YOU DON'T HAVE TO—
NONSENSE, PROTECTION IS IMPORTANT!

COUPLES!!

KLEINSKI
RICH GORANSKI © BE MORE CHILL
TIMOTHY KLEINMAN © DEAR EVAN HANSEN, MINE
R-RICHIE!
MWUAH
MY HAT DORK
S-STOP!
I HATE THESE FUCKING SCARS.
YOU'RE PERFECT TO ME, NO MATTER WHAT
T-THEY WERE SO M-MEAN!
DON'T LISTEN TO THEM, I LOVE YOU BABE

MELLMAN
JARED KLEINMAN
MICHAEL MELL
© DEAR EVAN HANSEN
© BE MORE CHILL
DUUUDE I HAVE A BELLY BUTTON!
ME TOO HOLY SHIT!!
← HIGH AF →
UHM.. JARE YOU DON'T HAVE TO CARRY ME-
NO I GOT THIS.
HEY, WANT SOME ICE CREAM?
SNIFF... Y-YEAH
MINE!

SKELLMAN
BENJAMIN KLEINMAN x GRAHAM SKELLY
BENHAM
I'M NOT A CHILD
COME ON. YOU WANT HIM! BUT I GUESS I'LL TAKE HIM BACK
NO HE'S MINE!
HEHEHEHE

I'M KING OF THE THEEEE!!
IN-INDEED YOU A-ARE!
8/11/18
AW, YOU GOT SOME ON YOUR BELLY, BABE!
MMMMH...
NOT... A WORD..
I MEAN ... I TOLD YOU TO PUT ON SUNSCREEN BABE
8/12/18

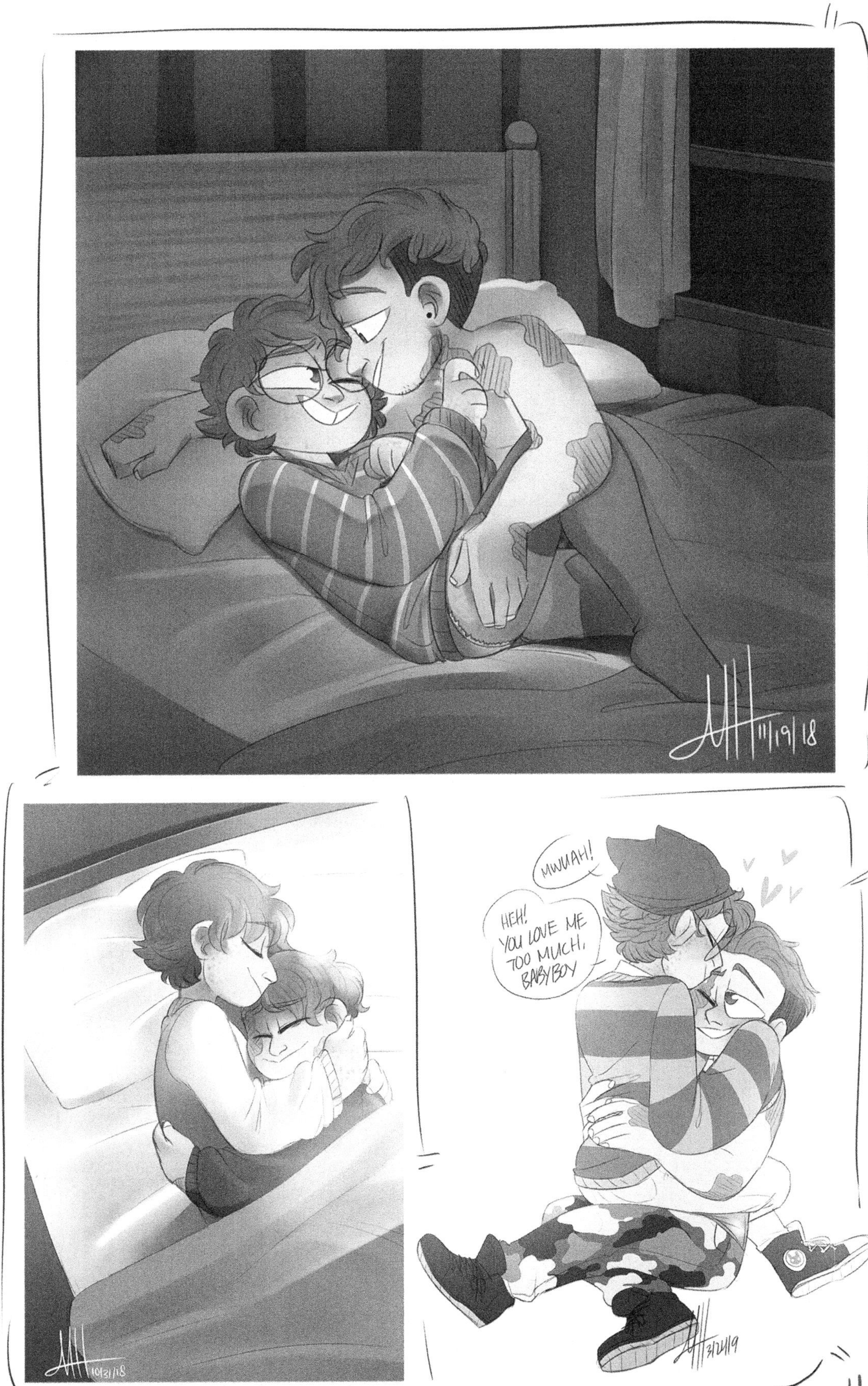
11/19/18
10/31/18
MWUAH!
HEH! YOU LOVE ME TOO MUCH, BABYBOY
3/2/19

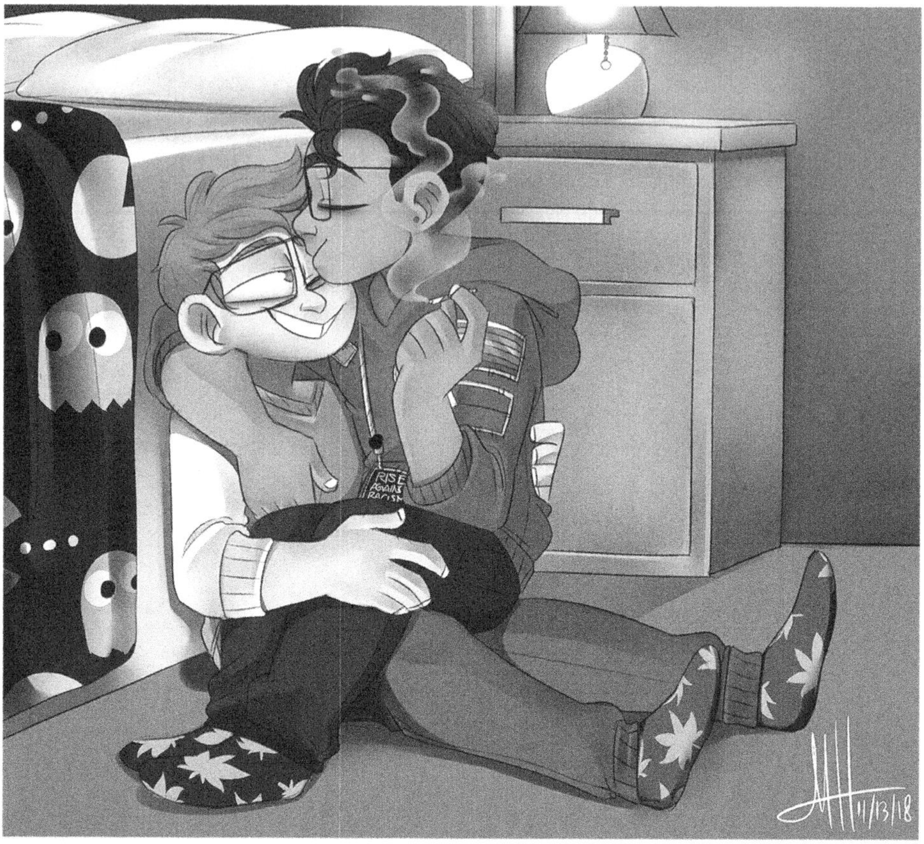
11/13/18

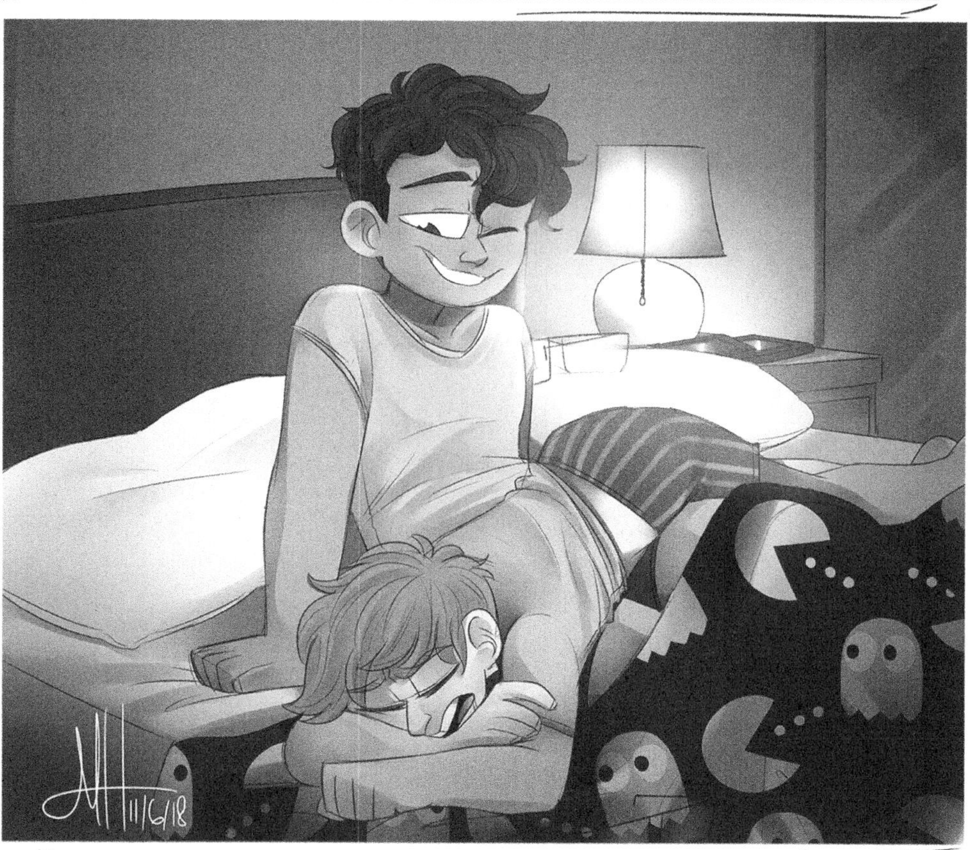
11/6/18

13

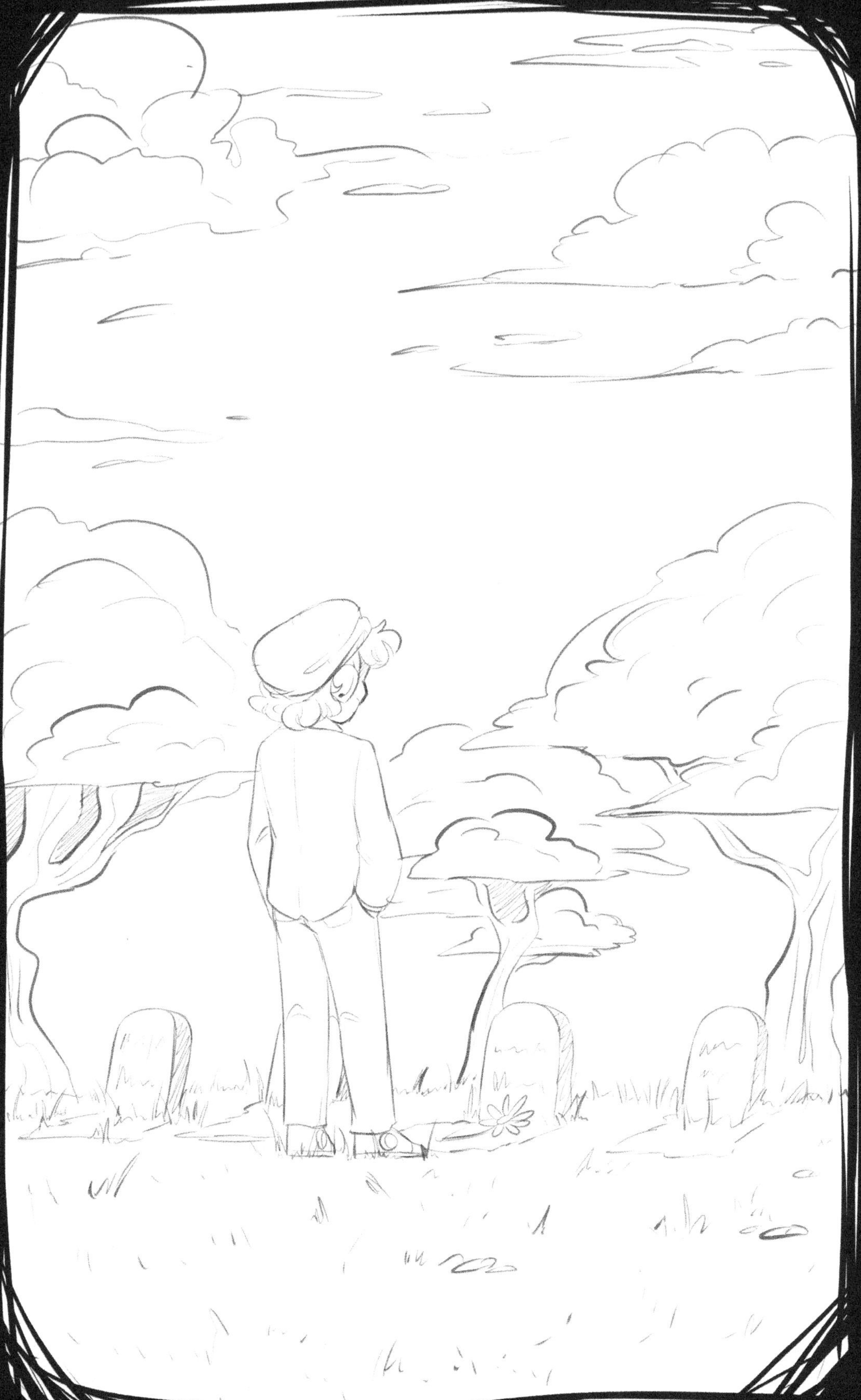

Dustin?...

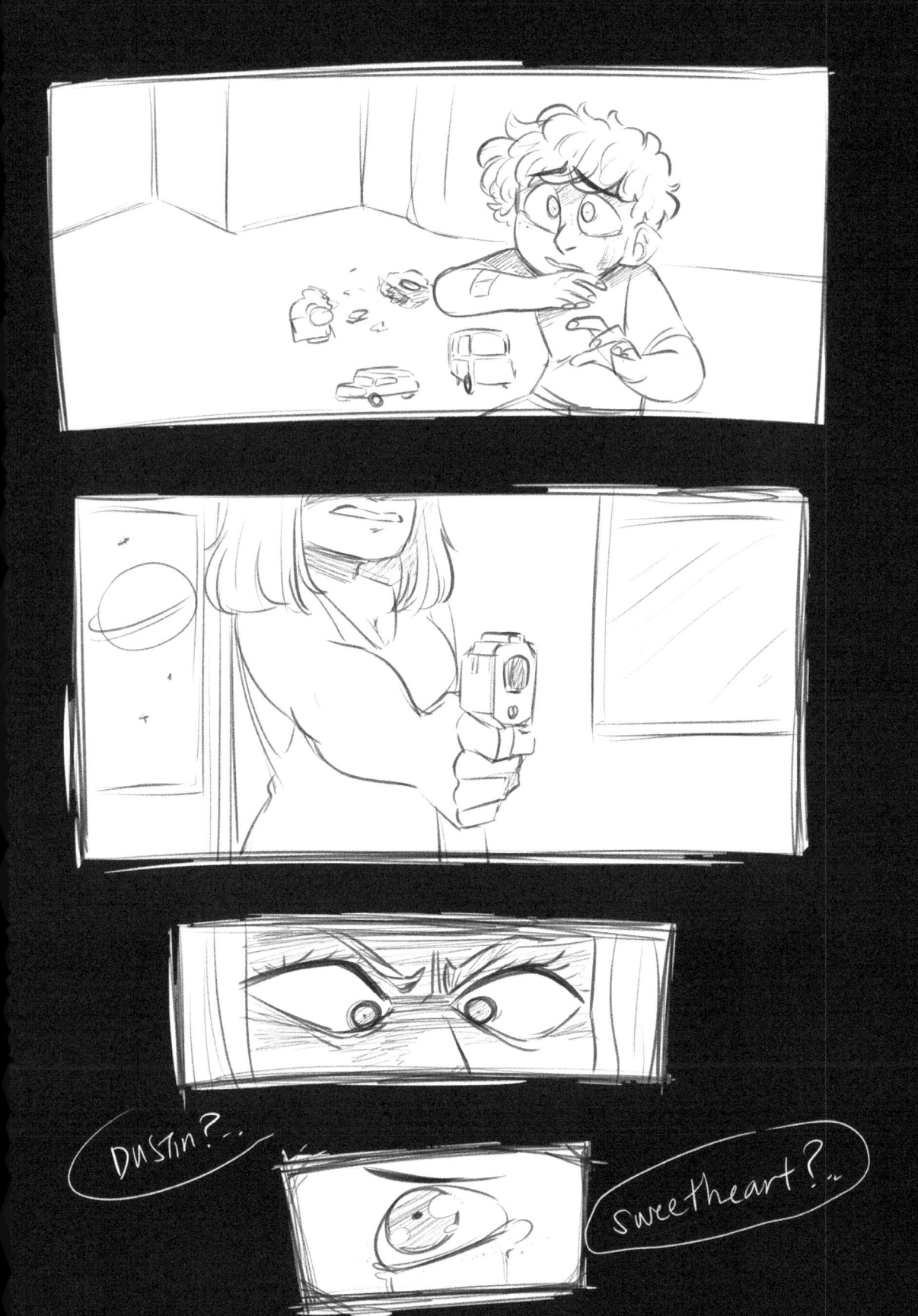

sweetheart?...

DUSTY?
LOOK WHO'S FINALLY HERE!
D-DADDY?
HAHA, Y-YEAH KIDDO, IT'S ME..!
DADDY!!
YEAH HEH! YOU'RE OKAY, THANK GOD, Y-YOU'RE OKAY!

YOU HAVE A LOT TO EXPLAIN.
YOU AND YOUR SON ARE IN A SAFE SPACE NOW.
IVE US THE WHOLE STORY.
I HAD TO STAY AWAY. I H-HAD NO.. NO CHOICE. SHE THREATENED.. TO KI-..
TO HURT HIM IF I TR-TRIED TO DEFEND—
SH... OKAY. BREATHE.

TIMMY, I NEED YOU STAY AND WATCH OVER DUSTIN, ALRIGHT?
I ASSURE YOU, HE'S A GOOD KID!
MMM... *SOFT WHIMPER*
AND HE REALLY NEEDS A FRIEND RIGHT NOW. UNDERSTAND?
..F..FRIEND.
YEAH! YOU TWO HAVE FUN, WE'LL BE RIGHT BACK.

aaa

20

21

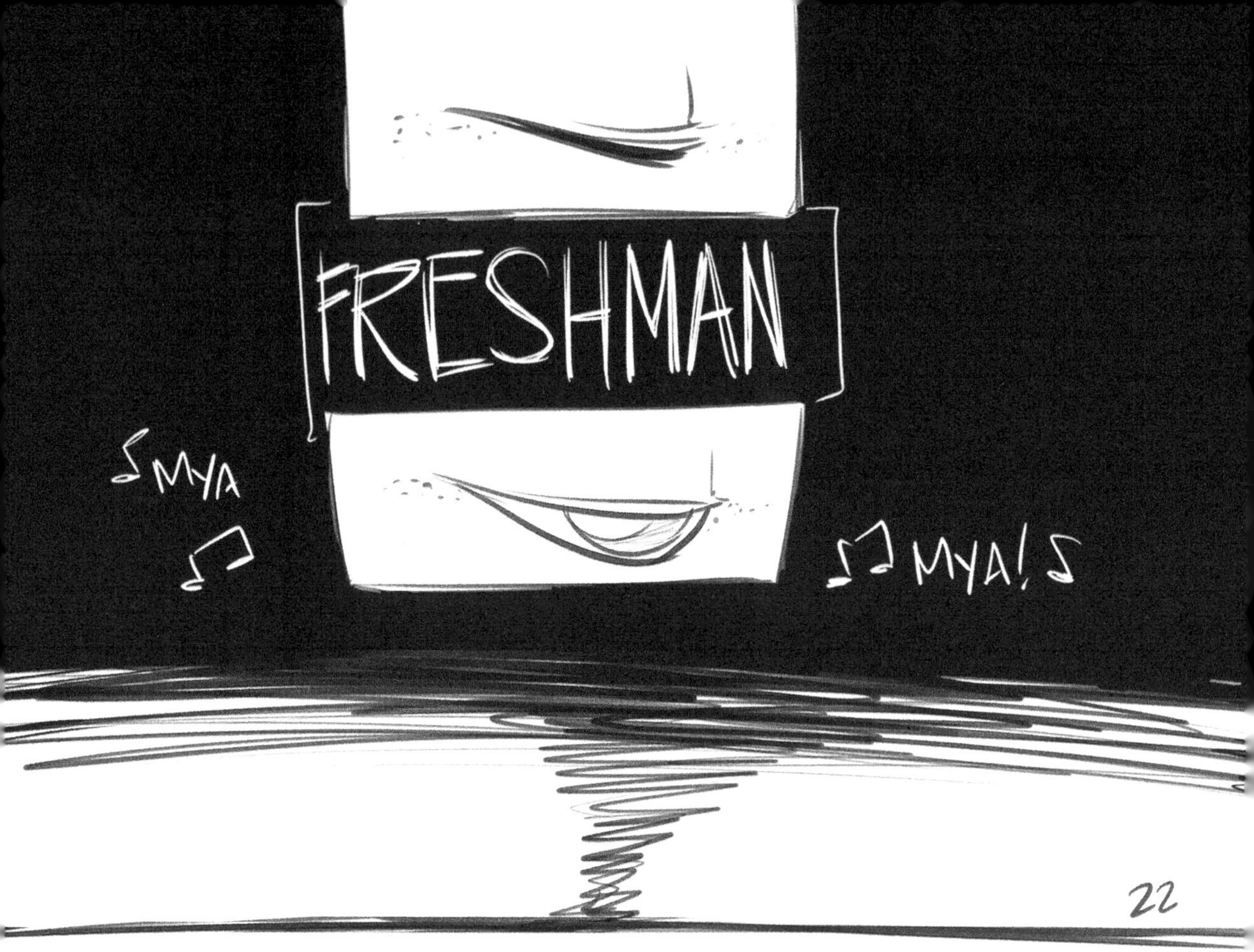

FRESHMAN
♪MYA ♪
♪♪MYA!♪

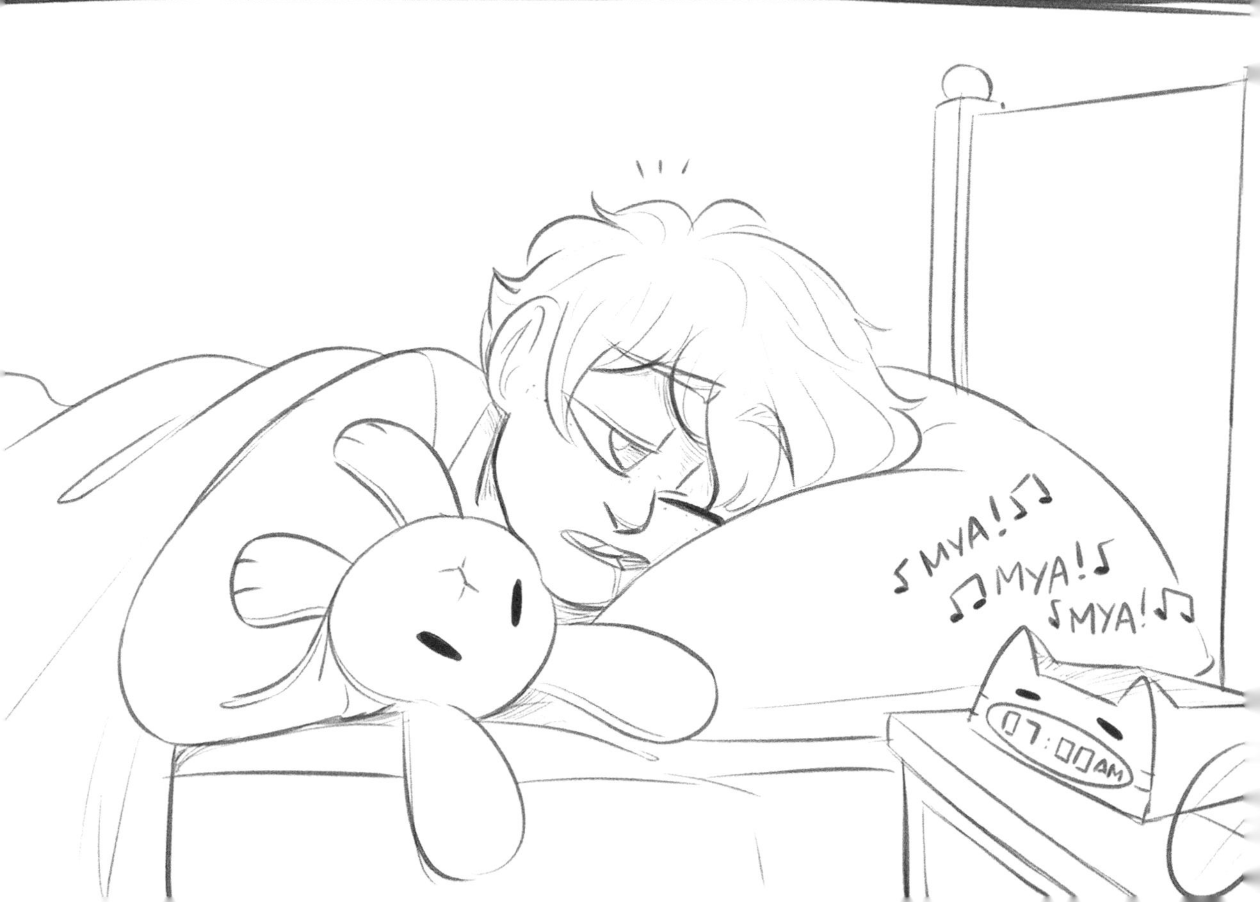

♪MYA!♪♪
♪♪MYA!♪
♪MYA!♪♪
07:00AM

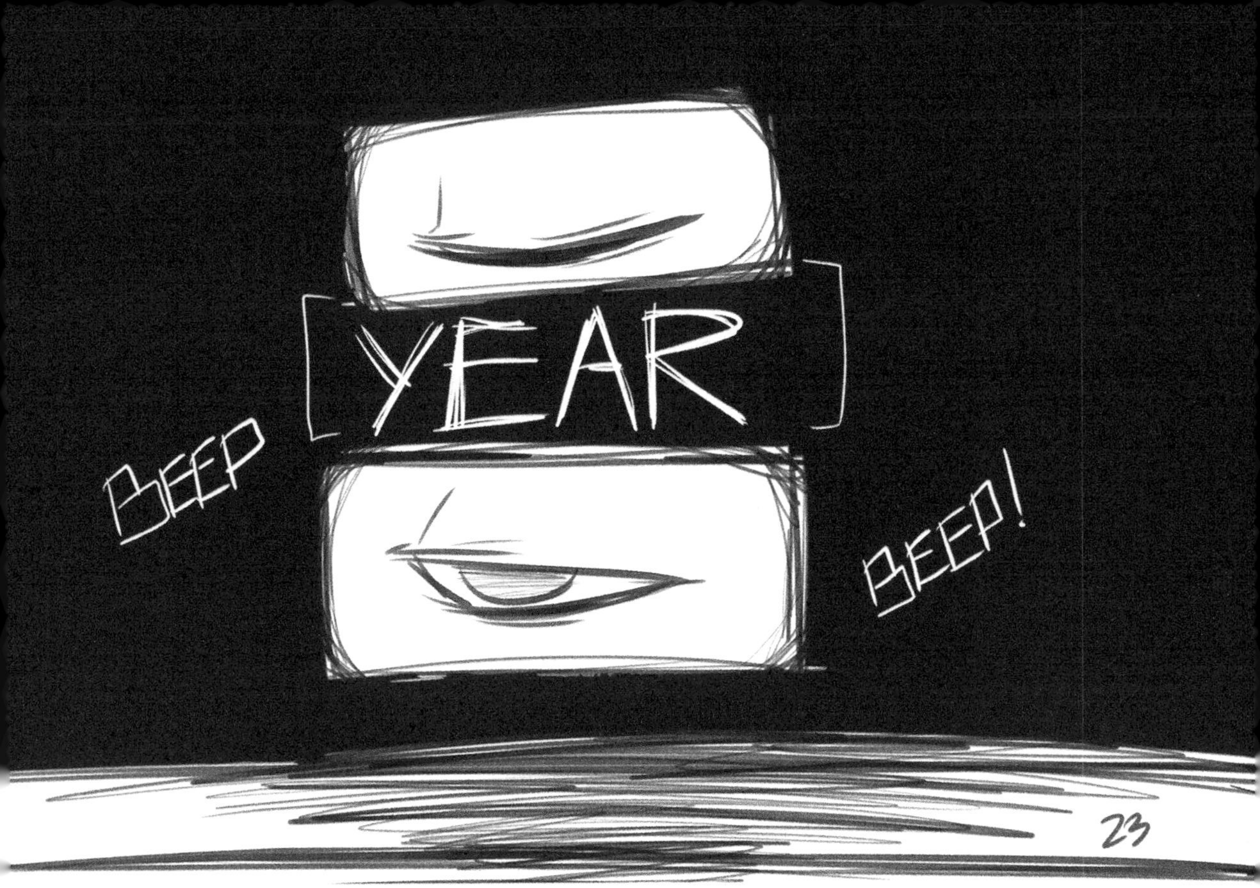
BEEP
YEAR
BEEP!

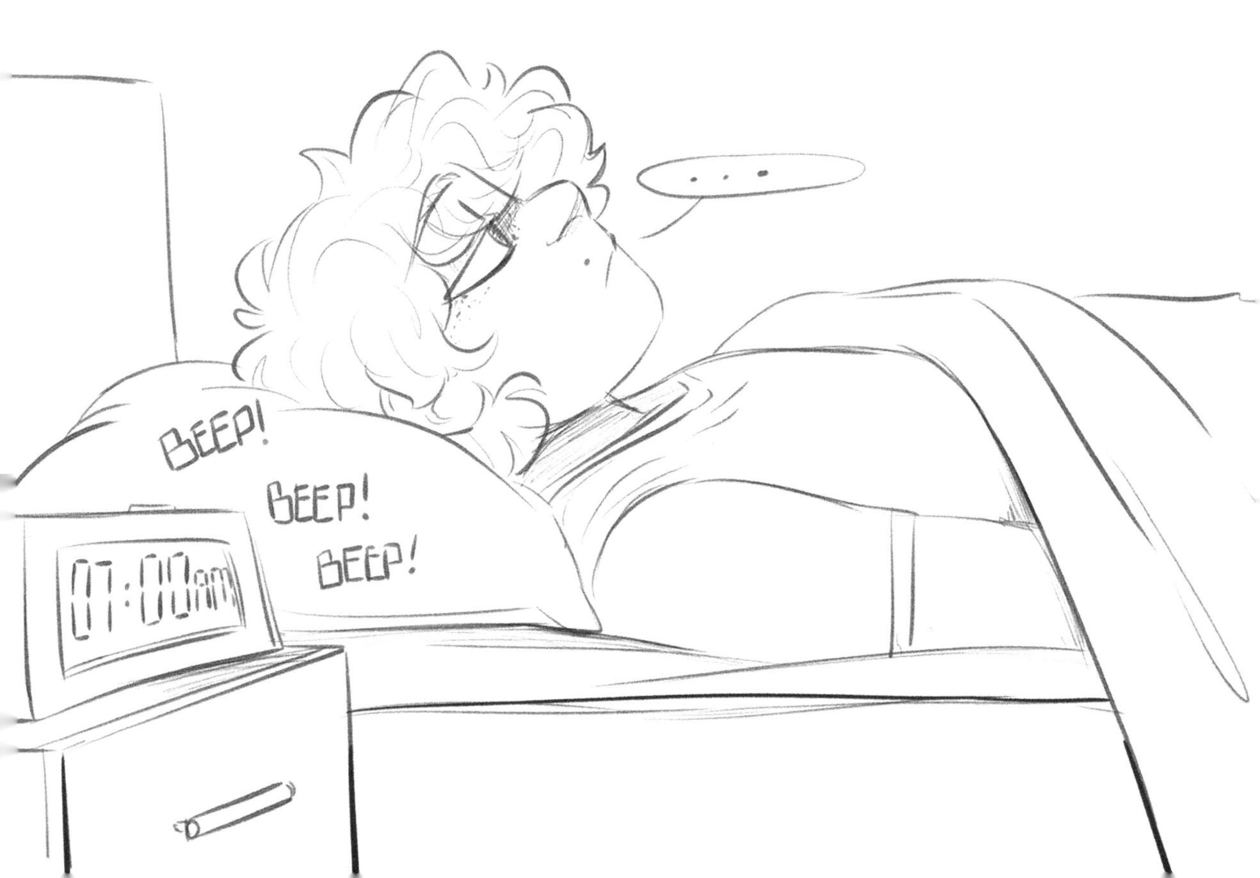
...
BEEP!
BEEP!
BEEP!
07:00am

24

25

26

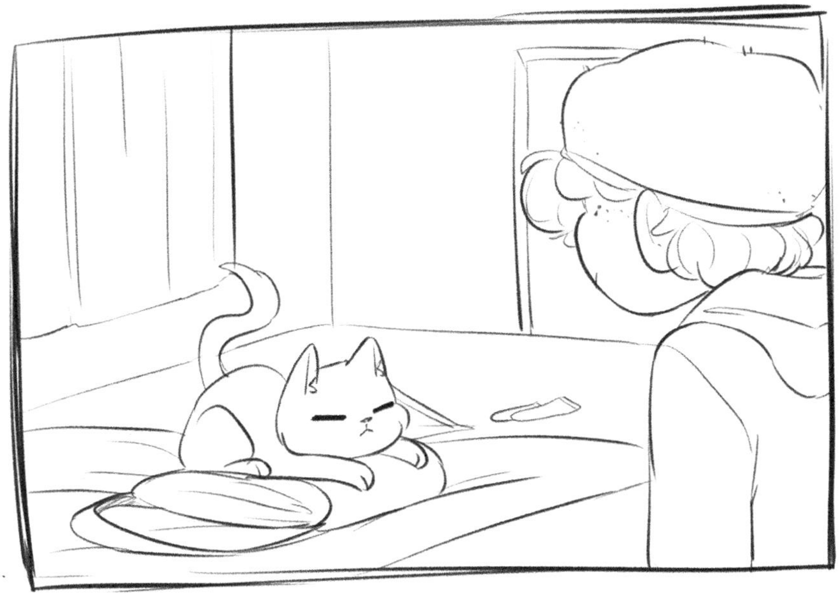
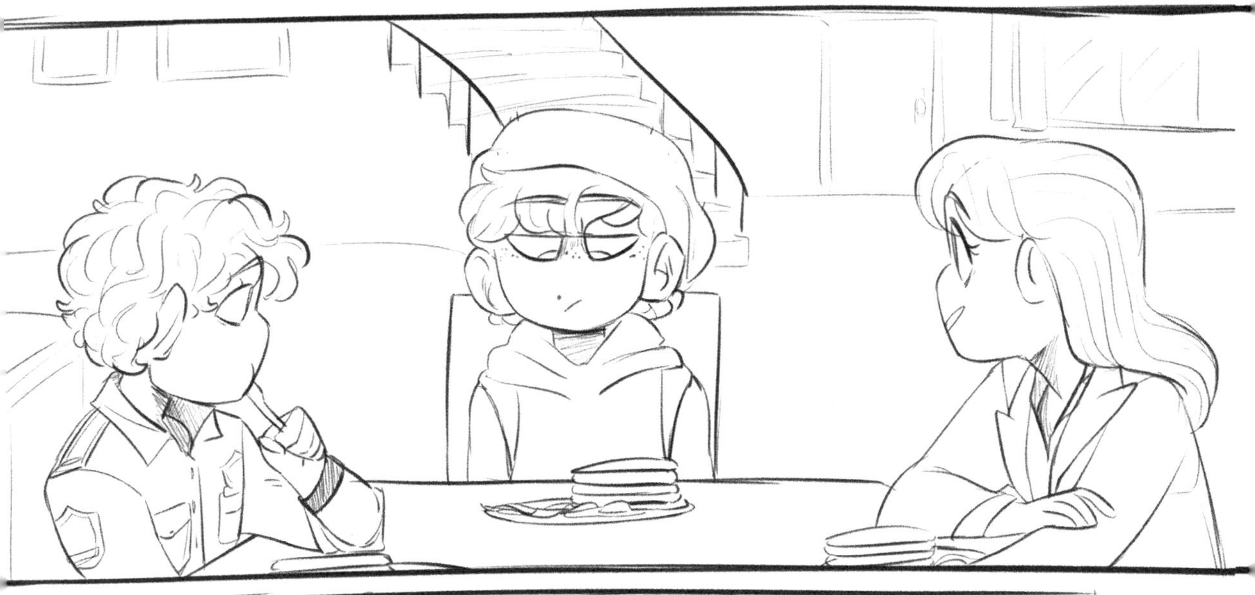
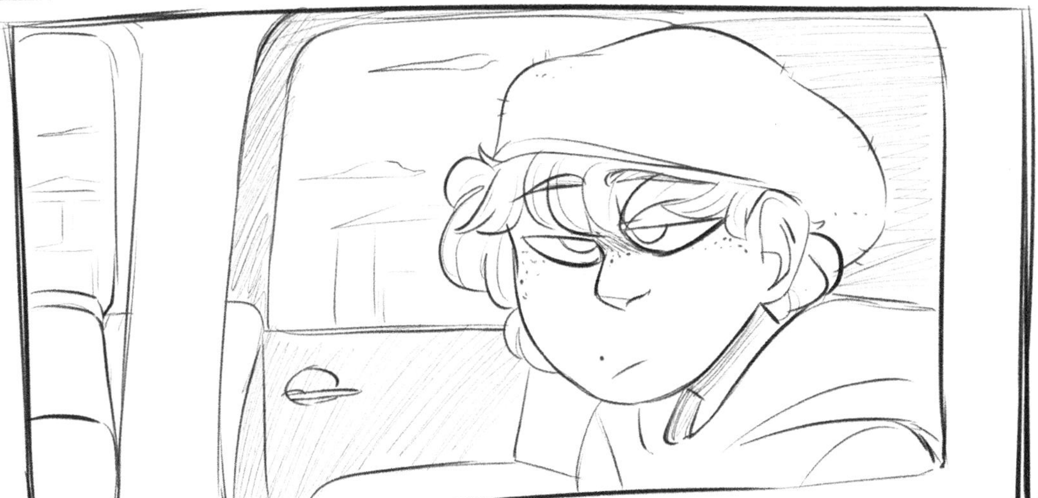

28

BACK OF SCHOOL

WELCOME TO JERSEY HIGH FRESHMEN!

BUMP!
aa!
mm!
AH!
OH UH.. SORRY, DIDN'T SEE YOU-
OH MY GOD... D-DUSTIN?!
OH, IS THIS HIM??

D... DU..
DUSTIN..?
...
UM.. HI—
DUSTY!!!
OHMYGOD
O-OHMYGOD
IT'S Y-YYOU!
IT'S B-B-BEEN
SO LONG!

YOU LLOOK S-STONED!
LONG TIME NO SEE, DUDE! FINALLY MOVED BACK INTO NEW JERSEY HUH?
UM.. AM I.. SUPPOSED TO KNOW YOU??
OH D-DO YOU NOT R-REMEMBER?
WELL IF IT HELPS, I'M JARED KLEINMAN. OLDER BROTHER, AND ADMIRER OF BATHBOMBS~
WELL HEH! YOU ALL NEED TO CATCH UP SOOO, I'LL GET GOING TO BIO—

NO WORRIES, I GOT YOU, FLOWER BOY.
YOU CATCH UP WITH DUSTBALL, KAY? SEE YOU LATER!
O-OKAY, CIAO!
...
H-HI, DUSTY. I'M T-TIMMMY. TIMOTHY K-K-KLEINMAN.

WE'VE BEEN B-BEST FRIENDS TH-THROOUGH CHILDHOOD! I M-M-MISSED YOU SO MMUCH WHEN Y-YOU MOVED OUT.

WE WERE... FRIENDS?

22nd JANUARY, 2006. AT M-MY BR-BROTHER BENJ-J-JI AND YOUR MMOM'S APARTMENT.. THAT SS-SMELLED LIKE LAVEN-LA-LAVANDER. WE W-WERE FOUR YEARSS O-OLD! IT WAS AWKWARD S-S-SILENCED AT F-FIRST, BUT WE PUSSHED YOUR BERRGUNDY TOY CAR BACK A-AND FORTH, THEN INTROD-D-DUCED OUR PLUSHES! RAFFY SMELLED L-LIKE MILK, AND YOU RREALLY LIKED B-BU-BUNNINGTON!

"R...RAFFY?..."

"Um... my memory's kinda fuzzy I don't really... remember.. sorry..."

WELL, IT W-WAS REALLY LLOONG AGO, AFT-AFTER ALL...
WILL Y-YOU BE FREEE FOR LUNCH?
WELL... SURE I GUESS??
OH OH OH! IDEA!!
THEN IT'S S-SE-SETTLED! LUNCH HOUR, I'LL T-TELL YOU EV-EVERYTHING. THAT GOOD?
HEH Y-YEAH.. GOOD, TIMMY.

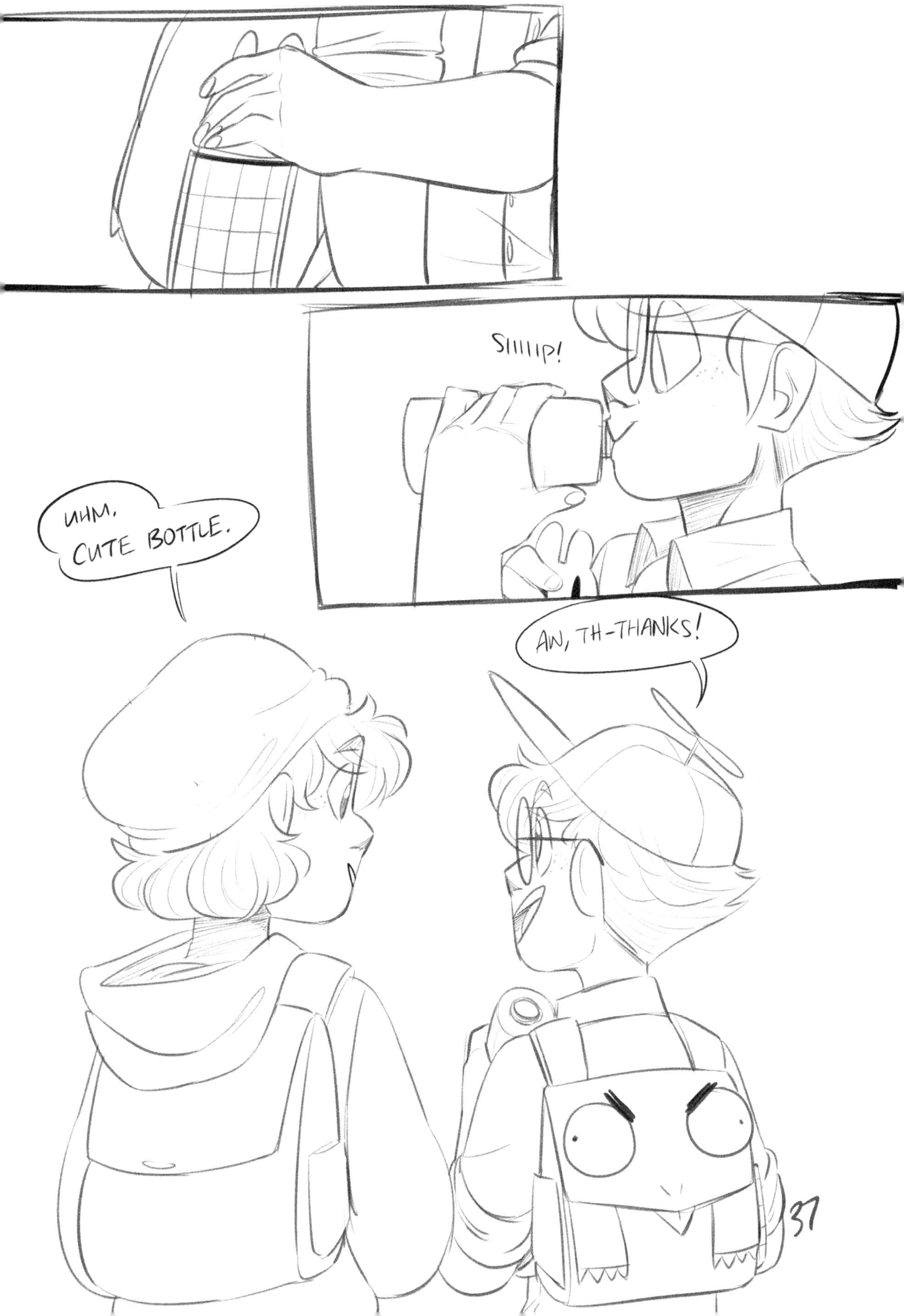
SIIIIp!
UHM, CUTE BOTTLE.
AW, TH-THANKS!

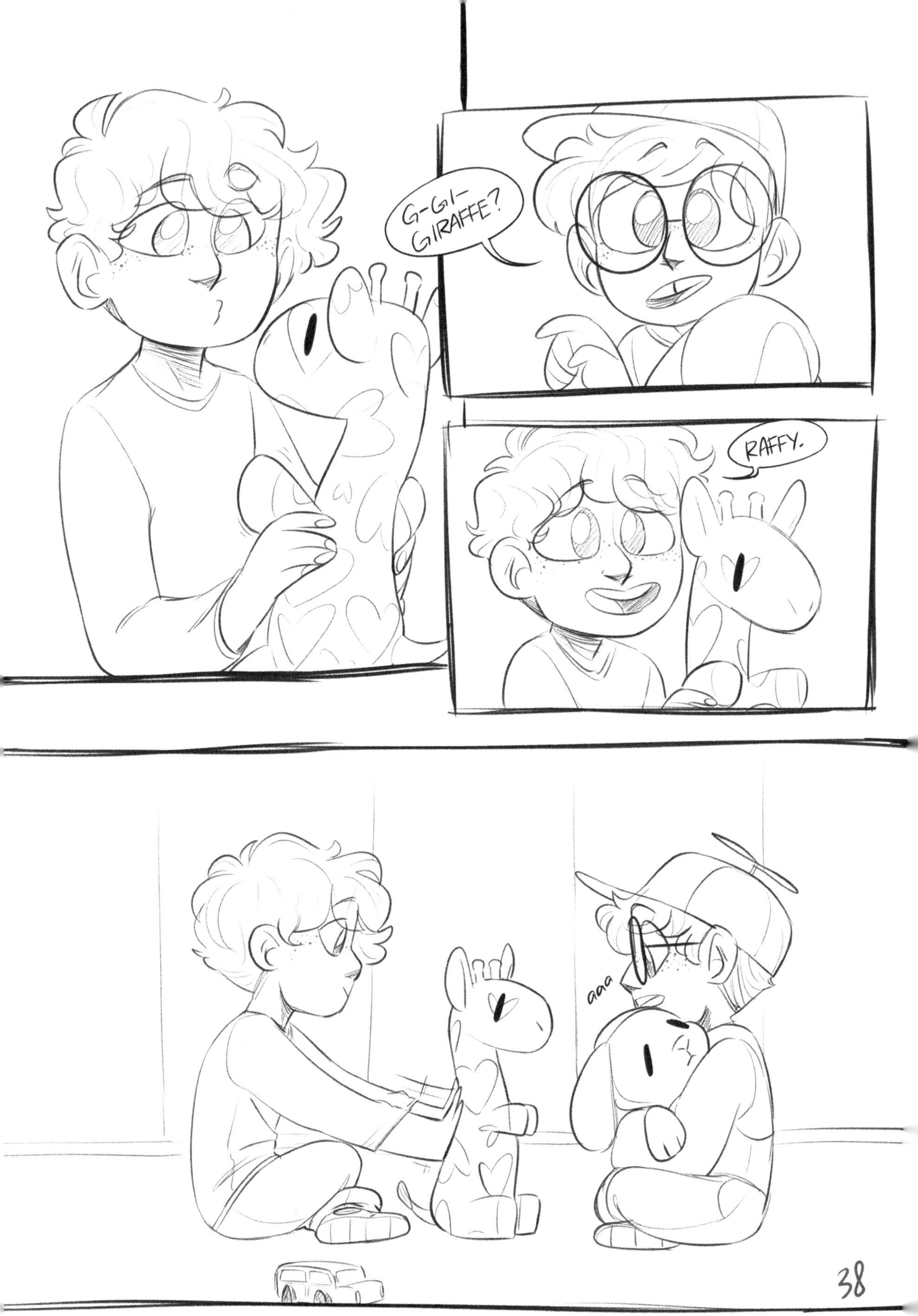
G-GI-
GIRAFFE?
RAFFY.
aaa

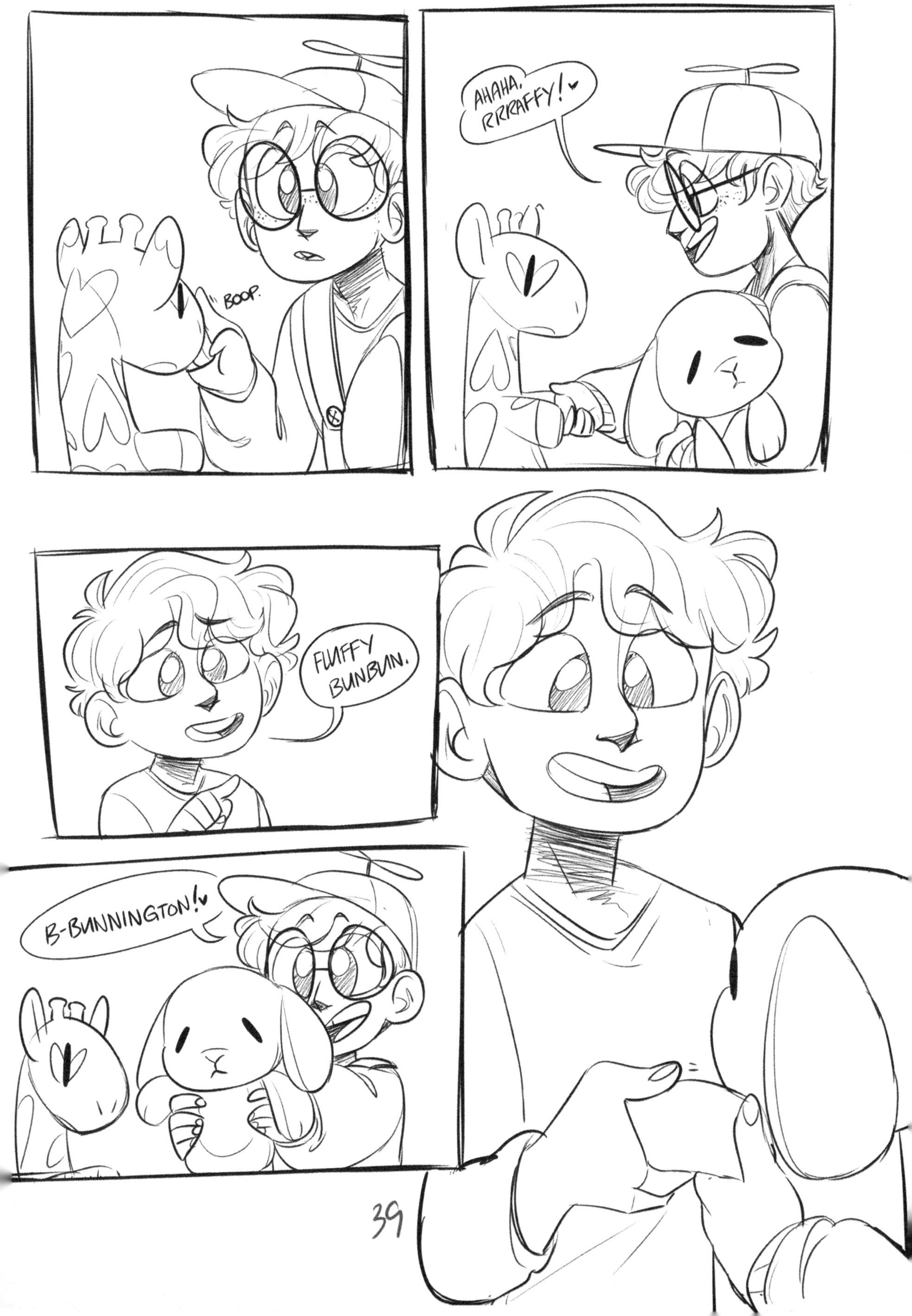
BOOP.
AHAHA, RRRAFFY!♥
FLUFFY BUNBUN.
B-BUNNINGTON!♥

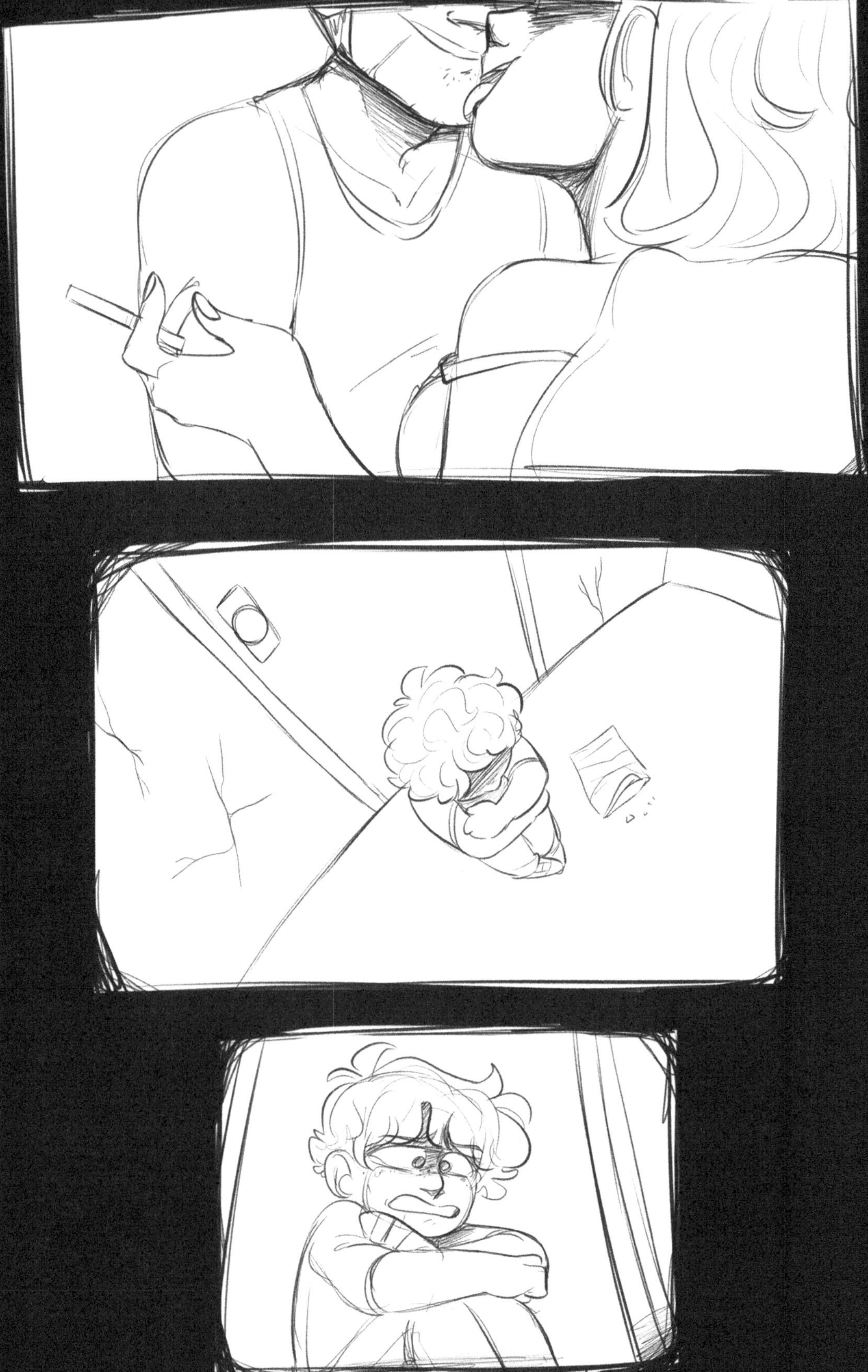

H-HEY!
POKE
YOU SURE LIKE SURPRISING PEOPLE.
YEAH HA, S-SO YOU R-RE-READY?—
HEY DUST! OVER HERE!
...JA-J-...

UH YEAH SORRY, I SHOULD GO OVER THERE BUT.. ARE YOU FREE AFTER SCHOOL?.. TIM?

UM.. YEAH... AFTER SSCHOOL.

ARIGHT, COOL. SEE YA SOON.
C-COOL, WHATVESS.
OH, TIMMY... ACTUALLY, CAN I BE LEFT ALONE FOR A BIT? I'M NOT FEELING SO... GOOD.
HEY, EVY!... L-LUNCH?

...OH!

A-ARE YOU SURRE YOU D-D-DON'T WANNA TALK ABOUT I-IT?

Y-YEAH, I'M SURE. WELL, I-I'LL BE AT THHE NEXT TA-TABLE IF YOOU NEED A-ANY-ANYTHING, OK?

THANKS, TIM...

44

MUNCH *MUNCH*

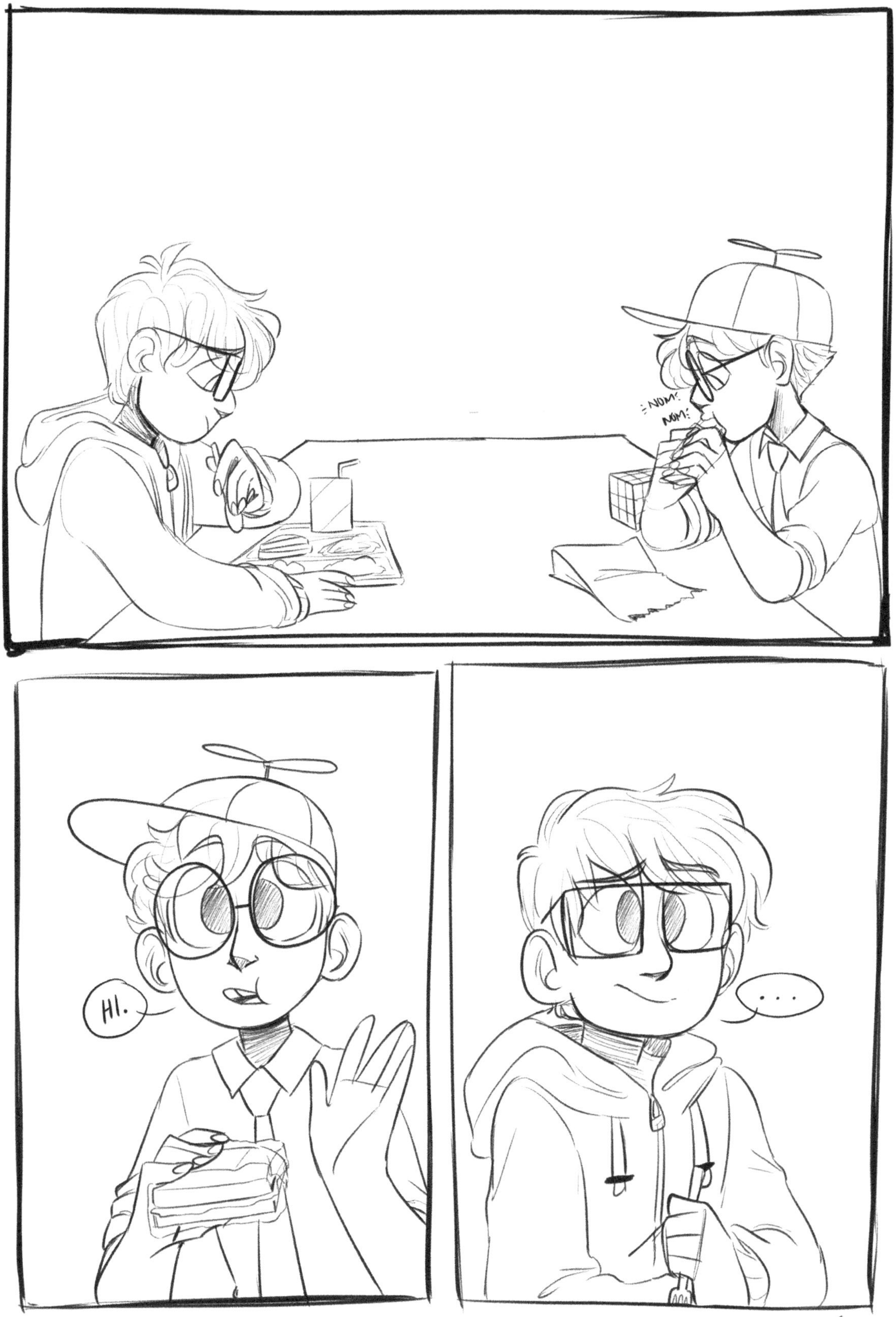
NOM
NOM
HI.
...

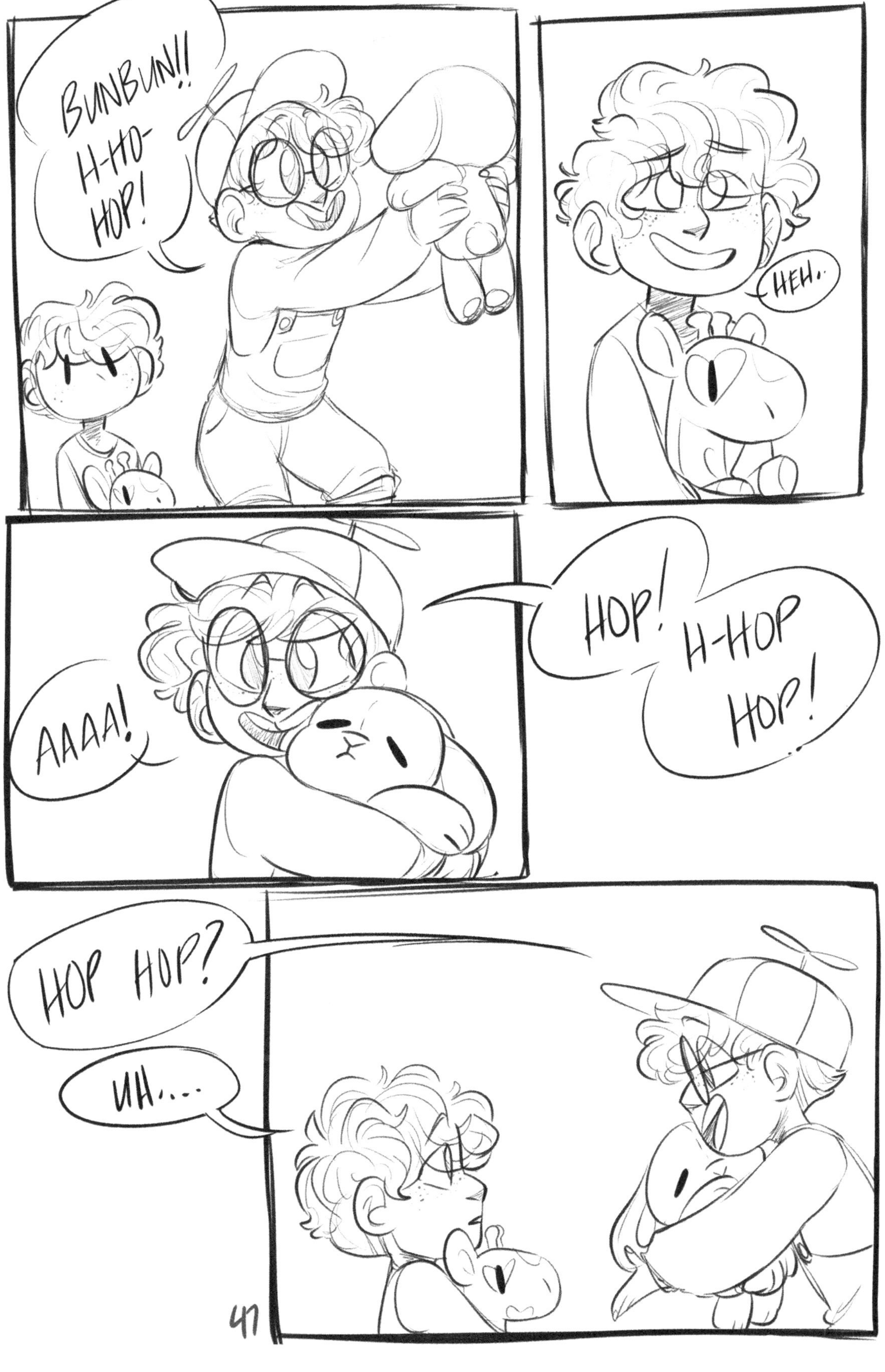
BUNBUN!! H-HO-HOP!
HEH..
HOP! H-HOP HOP!
AAAA!
HOP HOP?
UH....

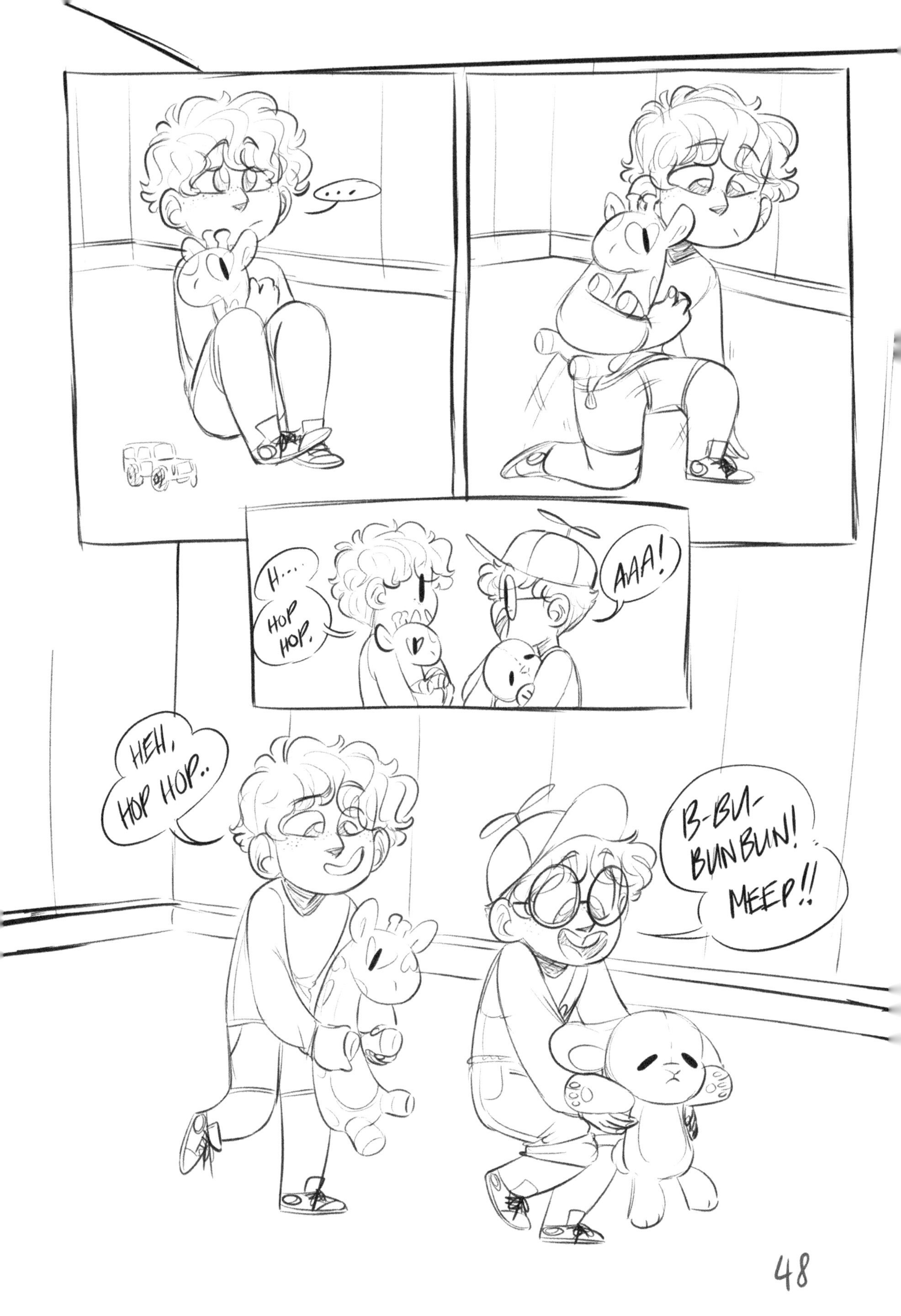
...
H....
HOP HOP.
AAA!
HEH, HOP HOP..
B-BU-BUNBUN! MEEP!!

HEY, WE'LL DO WHATEVER WE CAN TO PROTECT YOU BOTH, ARIGHT?
... OKAY.
FOR NOW, HOW ABOUT WE TREAT YOU AND THE KIDDO TO DINNER?
OH! YOU DON'T HAVE TO..
OH, WE KNOW. BUT WE WANT TO.
...I UH... THANK YOU.

HOW DO YOU BOYS FEEL ABOUT BURGERS?
B-BURJER!
IT'S BUR-GER, SWEETY.
B-BUR.. BURRGER.
THAT'S RIGHT, TIMTIM!
RIGHT!

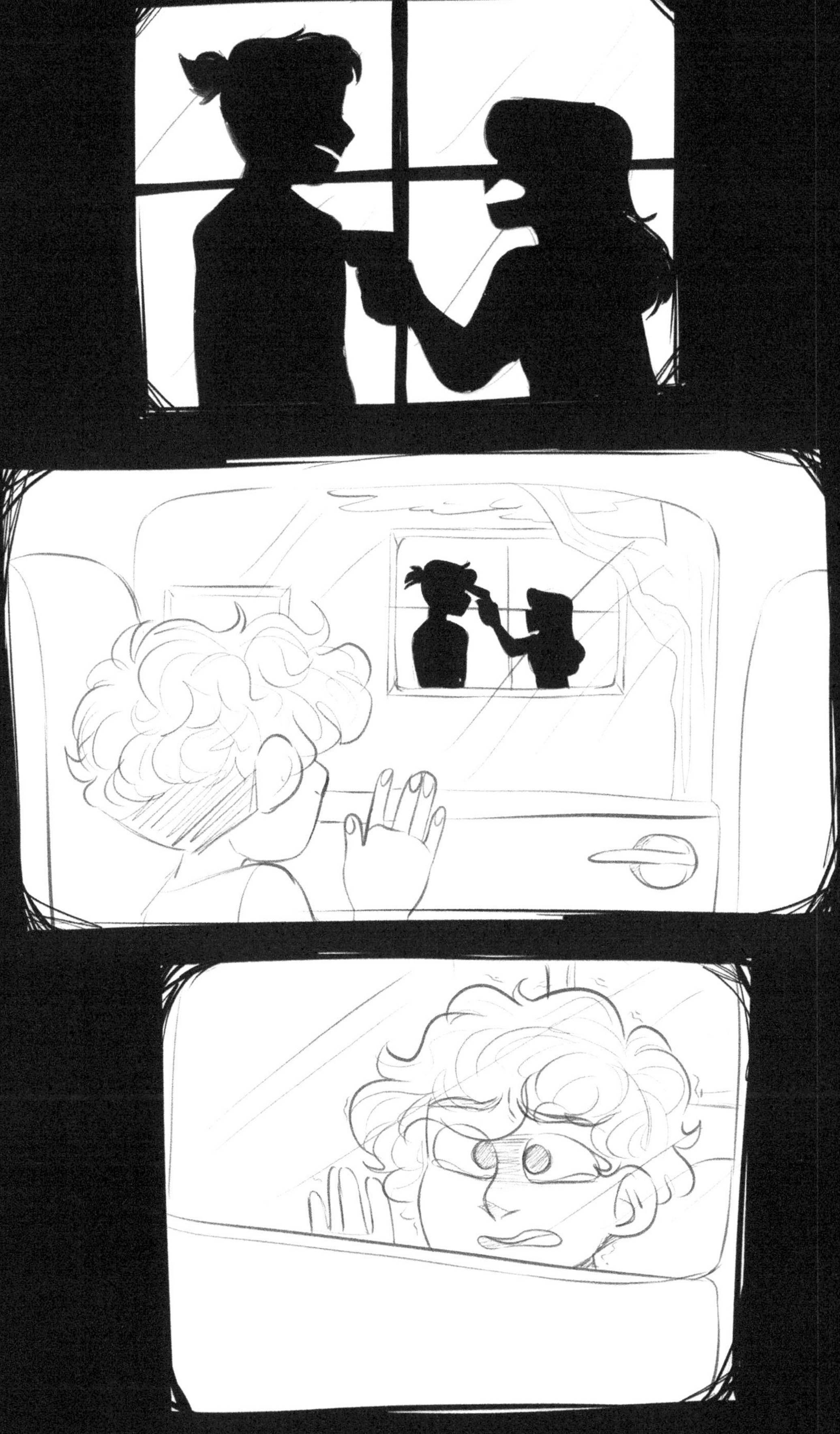

AAAAND, H-HERE WE ARE!

THE K-KL-KLEINMAN HOUSHOLD!

HUH... COMFY.

CHEZST-STICK?

"OH WELP, I'M NOT HUNGRY BUT... SURE. THANKS."

"T-THIS WAS THE FFFIRST SNACK WE SH-SHA-SHARE TOGETHER!"

"YOU L-LOOKED HUNGRYY."

"OH. I WAS, HUH?—"

"TIMMY, WELCOME HOME! I'VE FED SWEET LITTLE WAFFLES BEFORE LEAVING FOR WORK."

"OH, IS THAT A FRIEND OF YOURS?"

"IT'S DUS-DUSTIN, MA!"

"DUSSTY!! ♥"

...DUSTIN??
OH MY GOSH, IT'S BEEN SO LONG. TIMMY HAS SPOKEN SO MUCH ABOUT YOU! I HOPE YOU AND FAMILY ARE WELL.
AHA, WE'VE BEEN ALRIGHT MA'AM!
I'M REALLY SORRY I NEED TO HEAD TO WORK, BUT YOU TWO CATCH UP, OKAY?
LOVE YOU, DEARIE
I L-LO-LOVE YOU T-TOO, MOMMY!
MMM!

SEE YOU NEXT TIME, DUSTIN!
HUH... YOUR MOM IS NICE.
Y-Y-YEAH, SHE'S THE BE-BEST.
NOW, TO MMY BEDR-RO-ROOM!! MEEP!

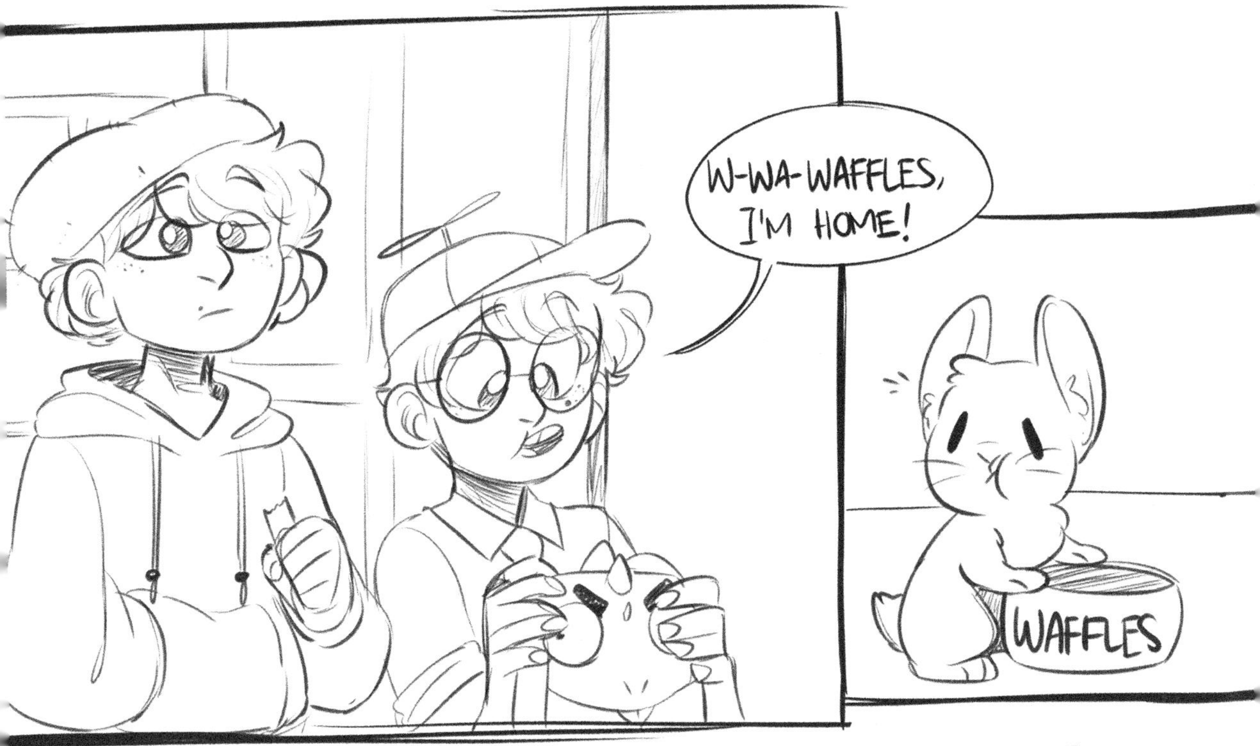
W-WA-WAFFLES, I'M HOME!
WAFFLES

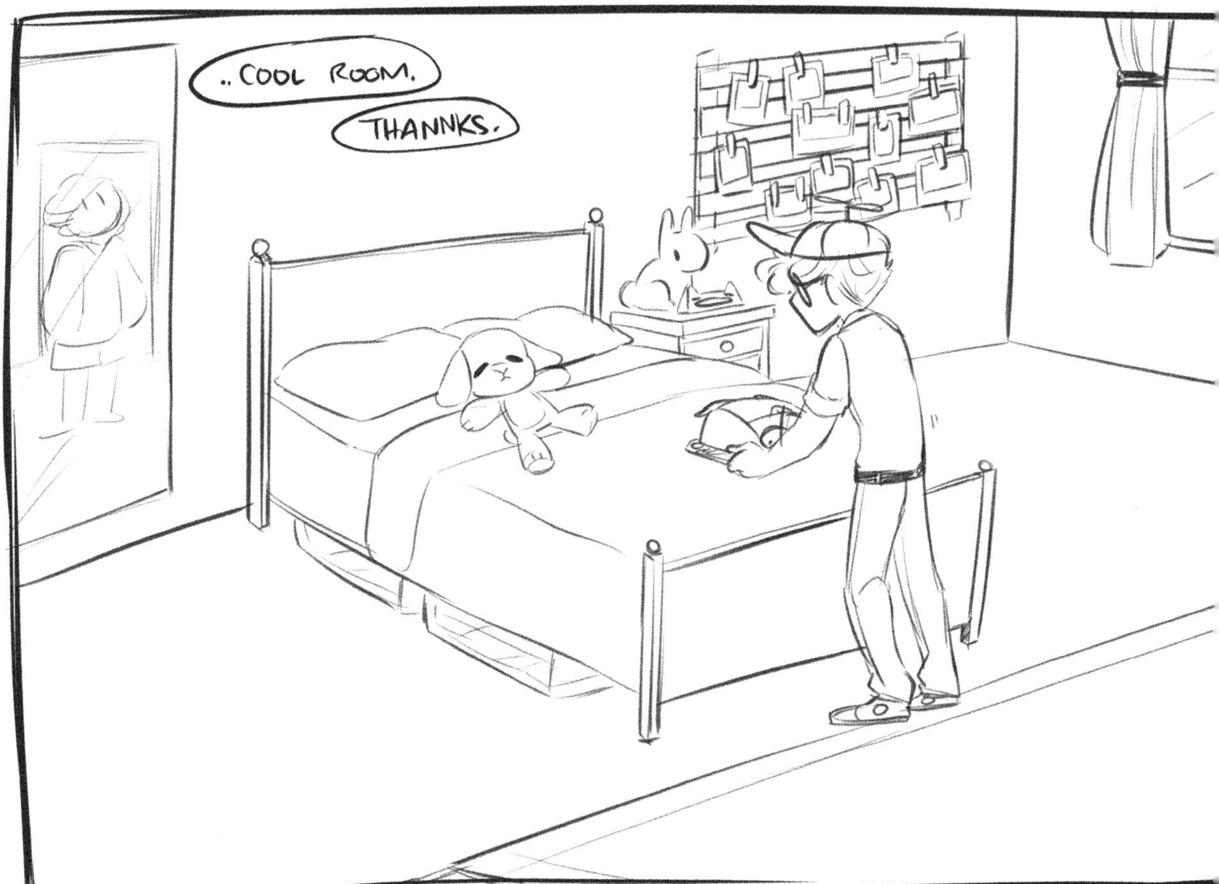
..COOL ROOM.
THANNKS.

HEY!

GIGGLE
I M-MISS YOU T-TO-TOO, LITTLE BABYY ♥

WHOA, THAT'S A LOT OF PHOTOS.

OH YEAH! I LO-LOVE KEEPING MEM-ME-MEMORIES.

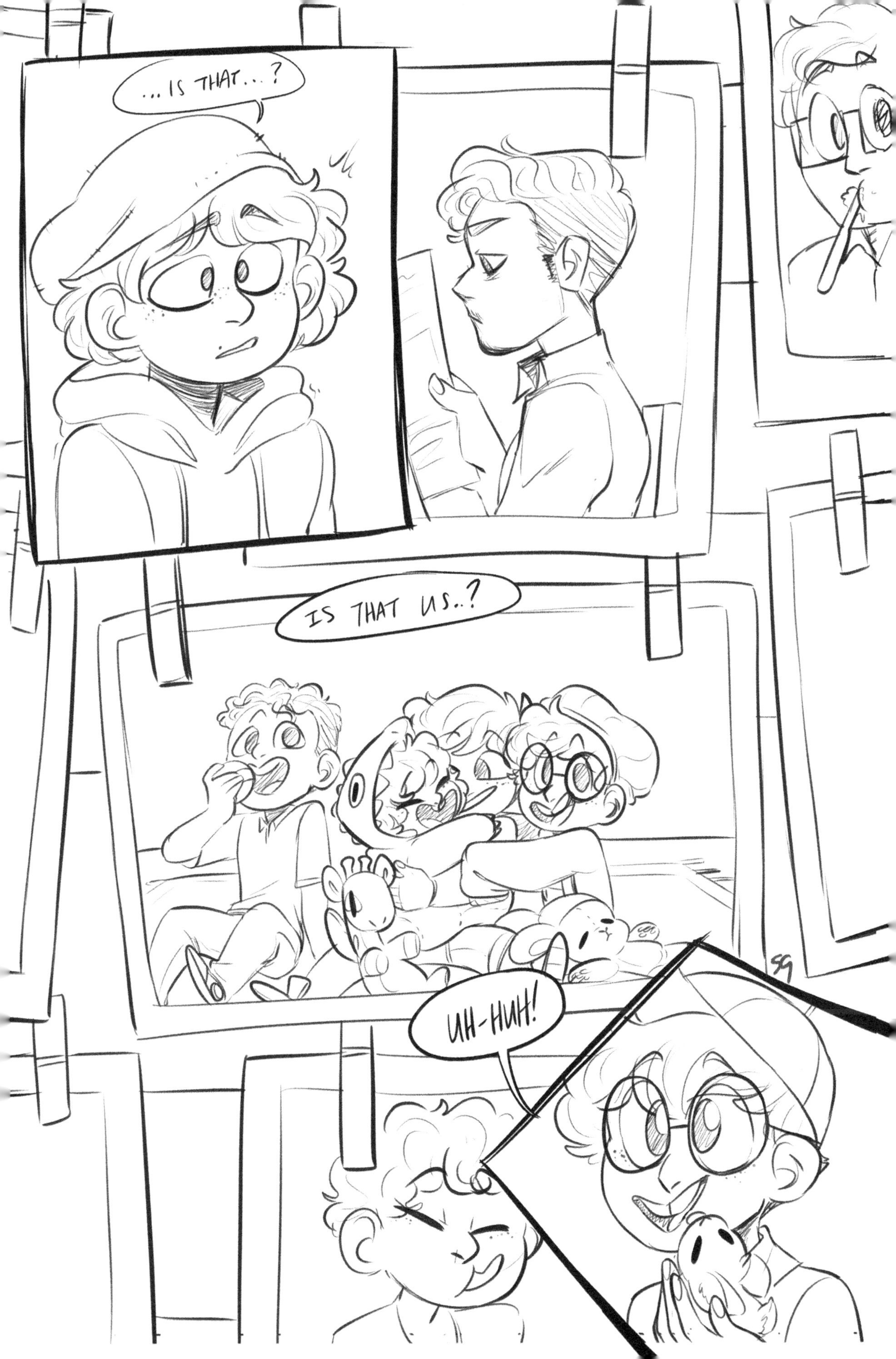
...IS THAT...?
IS THAT US..?
UH-HUH!

L-LIKE I SAID, INSEPARABLE. A C-COOL GANG!
I.. I WISH I COULD REMEMBER.. ..SORRY..
OH! O-OF COURSE!
MMAYBE RAFFY CAN H-HE-HELP!
60

!!

...you...

YOU KEPT HIM.. ALL THIS TIME??
BEFFORE Y-YOU AND THE F-FAM-FAMILY MOVED OUT, I GOT R-REALLY SSAD SO YOU L-LET ME KEEP RAFFFY.
OH, HEH.. PLEASE TELL ME MORE.
MEEP!! YES, YES I W-WILL!
W-WE HAVE ALL THHE TIME!

SO HEH, WELCOME TO MY HUMBLE ABODE.
NOT MUCH BUT, COZY, Y'KNOW?
GASP!

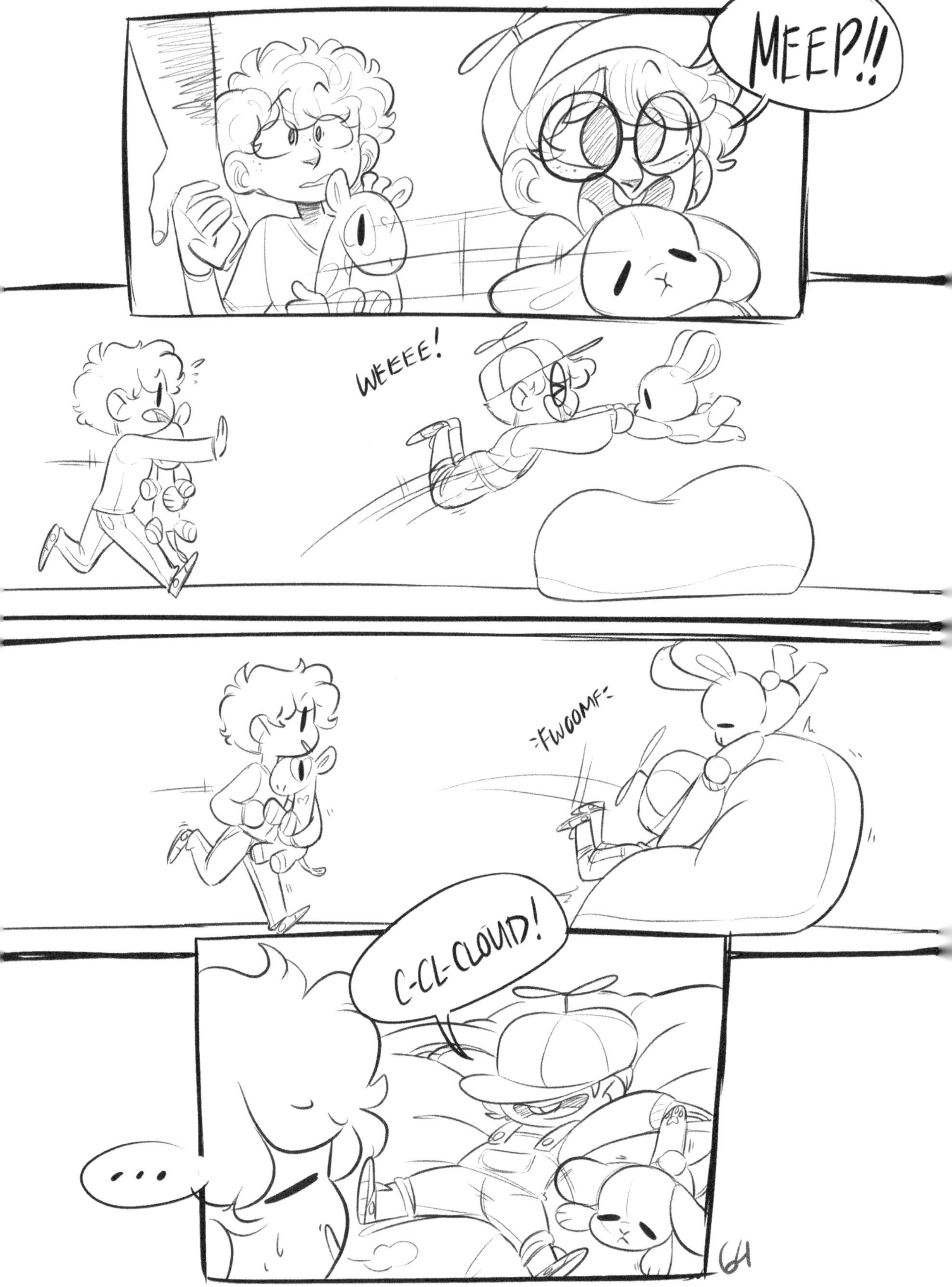
MEEP!!
WEEEE!
FWOOMF
C-CL-CLOUD!
...

"HUH, IT'S BEEN A WHILE SINCE HE LAST SMILED."

"YEAH, IT'S NICE TO SEE HIM WITH A FRIEND."

"WELL, EVERYTHING IS ALRIGHT. EXCEPT SOMEONE GOT HIMSELF A STOMACH ACHE FROM EATING THE WHOLE ICE CREAM."

"CALL ME A FATTIE AGAIN, I DARE YOU."

"WELL WHAT ABOUT YOU TWO? EVERYTHING ALRIGHT AT HOME?"

"HAHA! I MEAN YOU GOT QUITE THE APPETITE."

MAYBE WHEN WE GET MARRIED SOMEDAY..
COULD YOU VOW TO NOT TEASE ME?
NOT A CHANCE.♥
PPFT!♥
.....
OUT-OU-OUTSIDE!
MEEP MEEP!

67

HEY...

OH... HEY.

YOU O-OKAY?
YEAH.. SURE. MAYBE.
IT'S ALL G-GOING TO WORRK OUT.. BENJI IS D-DOING EVERYTHING HE C-CAN.
SHE'S.. SHE'S GOING TO GET THE PEACE SHE DESERVES—
GUYS, SHE.. WE CAN'T JUST HOPE THIS ALL WORKS OUT.
WE HAVE TO WIN THIS.
WE NEED TO WIN THIS.

CAUSE WHEN WE DO...

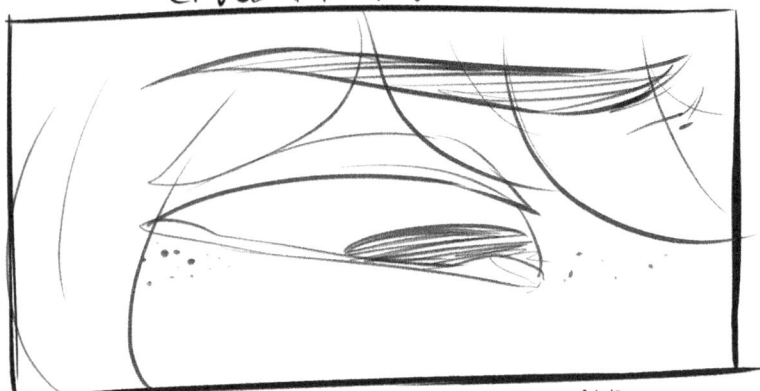

I COULD.. FINALLY LOOK FOWARD.. AND..

SHE WOULDN'T HAVE TO WORRY ABOUT ME ANYMORE...

SOB
SOB

COMPILATION OF OLD BMS COMICS

> SOME COMICS MAY NOT BE CONSIDERED CANON ANYMORE BECAUSE OF CHANGES, BUT I HOPE THIS IS A NICE TRIP TO THE PAST! MOST OF THEM OTHERWISE ARE A PART OF THE STORY.

HEY. BABE! YOU LOOK DIFFERENT.
??
IT'S CUTE!
!?!
NEVER KNEW YOU LIKED PROPELLER HATS.
I'M F-FLATTERED BUT I LIKE S-SOMEONE ELSE.

!!
RIGHT HERE, CUTIE~
HI!
-SNICKER-
-SNICKER
HI!
-SNICKER
-SNICKER

YO, EARTH TO LIL BRO!
HUH WHA?!
CLICK
CLICK
SOMEONE ON YOUR MIND?
N-NO!?
MAYBE?
WHAT WERE YOU WRITING IN YOUR BOOK?
HEY, S-STOP IT!!
AW COME ON, ONE PEEP!
I-IT'S NOTHING I S-SWEAR!
LET'S SEE WHO'S TIMMY KISSING ON A TREE WIIIITH~
I BET IS STILL ACORN!
EVAN AND I ARE JUST FRIENDS YOU KNOW THAT GIVE BACK MY BOOKAAA
LET'S SEE WHO'S TIMMY KISSING ON A TREE WIIIITH~
I BET IS STILL ACORN!
EVAN AND I ARE JUST FRIENDS YOU KNOW THAT GIVE BACK MY BOOKAAA
MR. RICHIE KLEINMAN
HE HIGH FIVED ME TODAY.
I AIN'T WASHING MY HAND. EVER!!!
RG + TK
RICH!?!
THUP?
. . . . .

HOO BOY. I MESSED UP. BAD.
HEY. HERE'S SOME CRAZY ADVICE: DON'T. CHEAT. EVER???
I D-DIDN'T MEAN IT, IT WAS AN A-ACCIDENT!
SO, BASICALLY YOU RODE YOUR BIKE AND SUDDENLY FELL INTO HER VAGINA.
FINE, FINE. VALID POINT.
JUST ACCEPT IT. MICHAEL AND I WILL LET YOU STAY AT OUR PLACE TIL YOU GET YOUR OWN. AND A JOB.
S-SORRY WE'RE LATE!

I CAN SEE THAT
OH, BY THE WAY, THIS IS BENJI.
HI! YOU MUST BE RICH—
<3 TIMMYSSS
NAH, THERE'S MILLIONS OF YOU IN MY HEAD
!!
UGH, DUDE
...
R-RI-RICHIE!
SNICKER
SNICKER
SNICKER
YOU'RE LUCKY MIKEY'S NOT HERE TO KICK YOUR ASS.

75

WORK
WORK!!
BENJAMIN
WORK
WORK!!
JAAARED!
AND TIMTIM!
THE KLEINMAN BROTHERS!

77

78

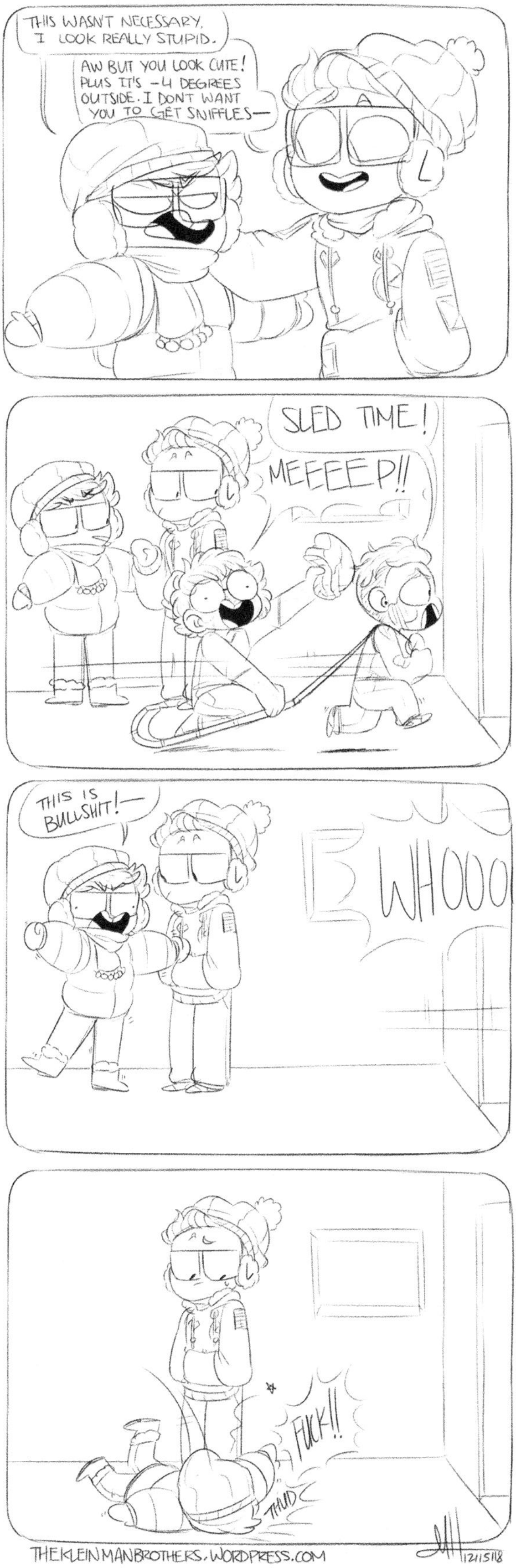

THEKLEINMANBROTHERS.WORDPRESS.COM

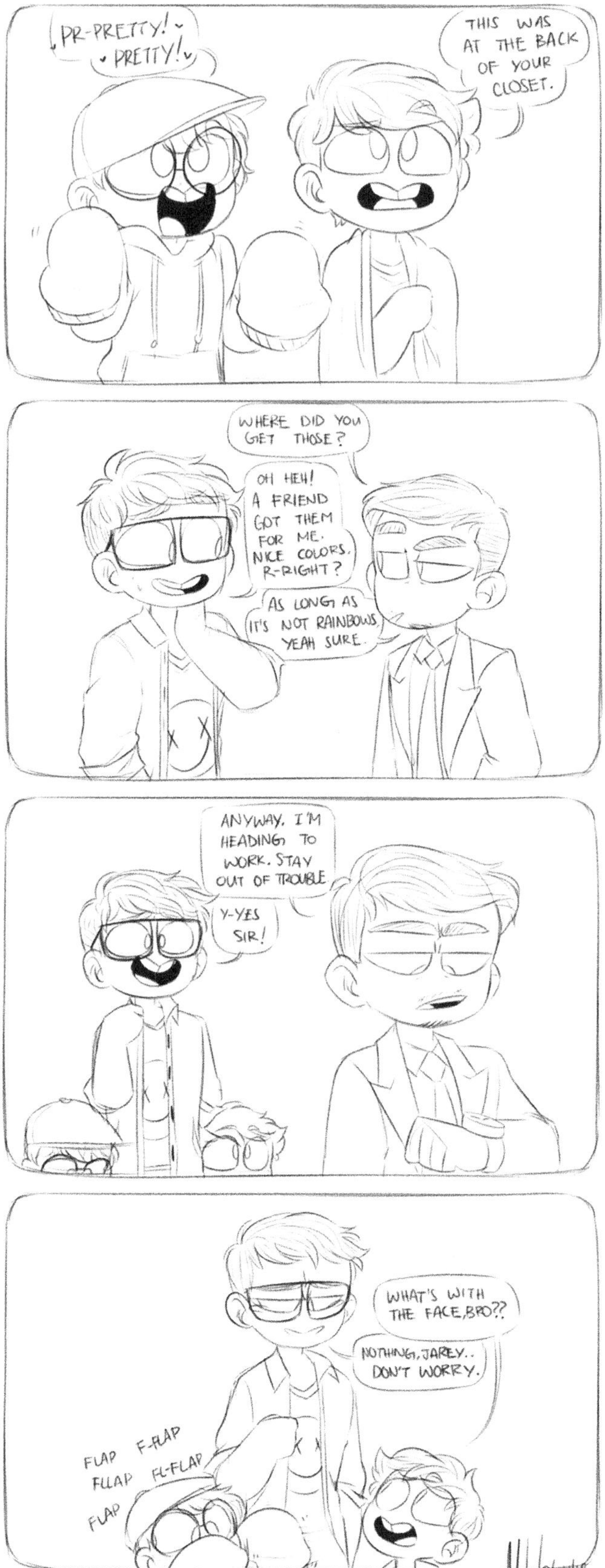

MADHATTEY.TUMBLR.COM
INSTAGRAM@MADHATTEY

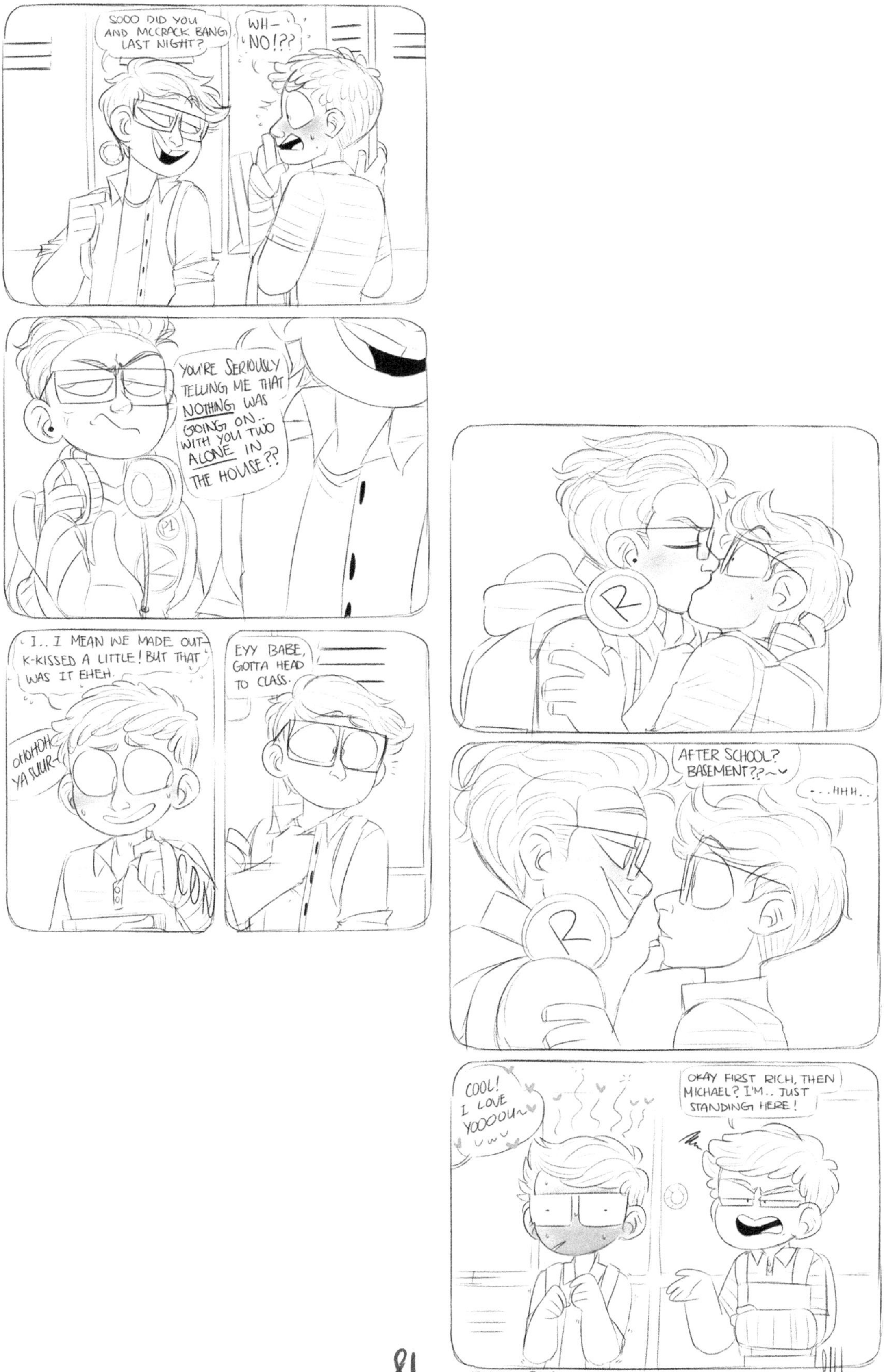

TUMBLR@MADHATTEY
INSTAGRAM@MADHATTEY

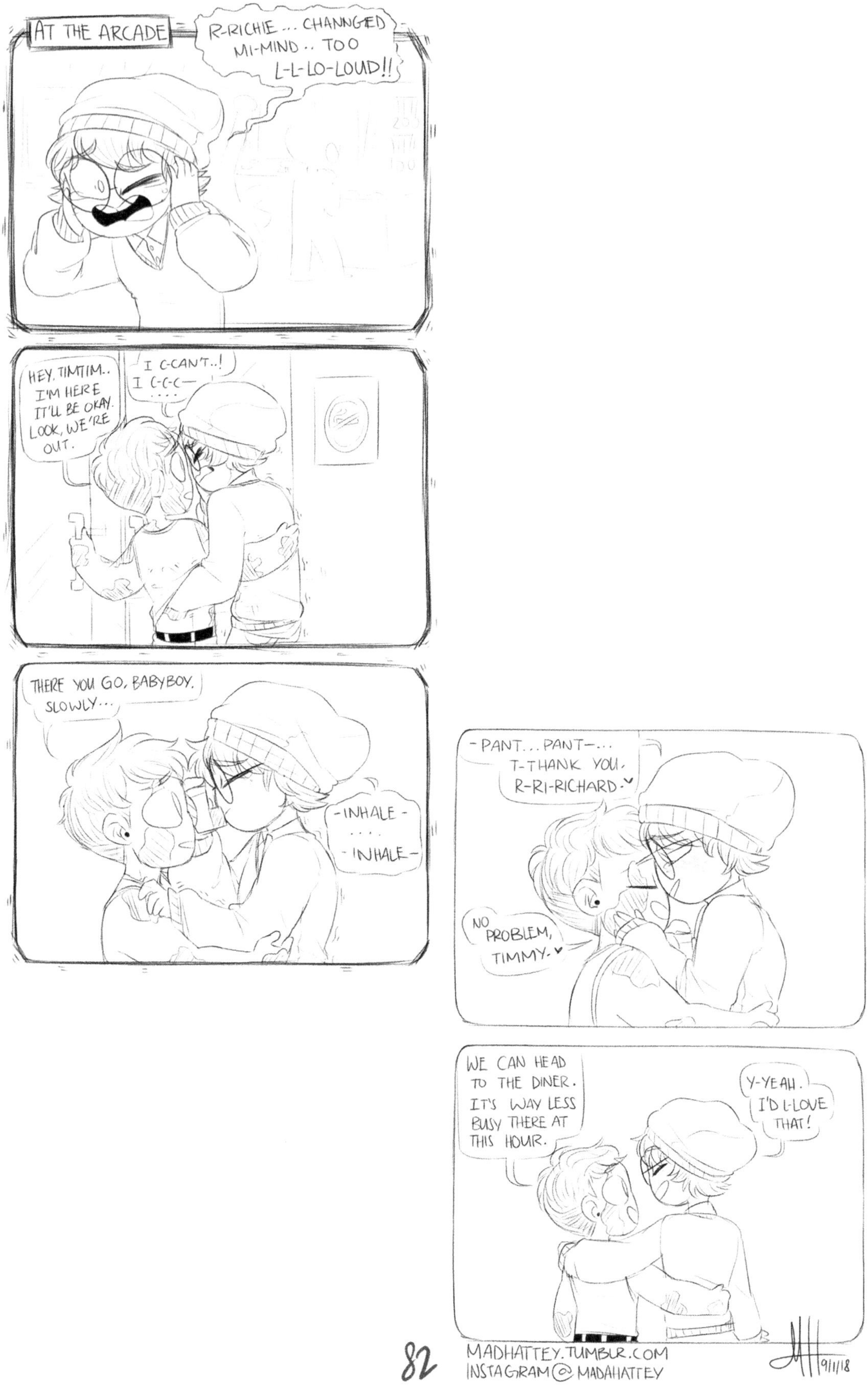

MADHATTEY.TUMBLR.COM
INSTAGRAM @ MADAHATTEY

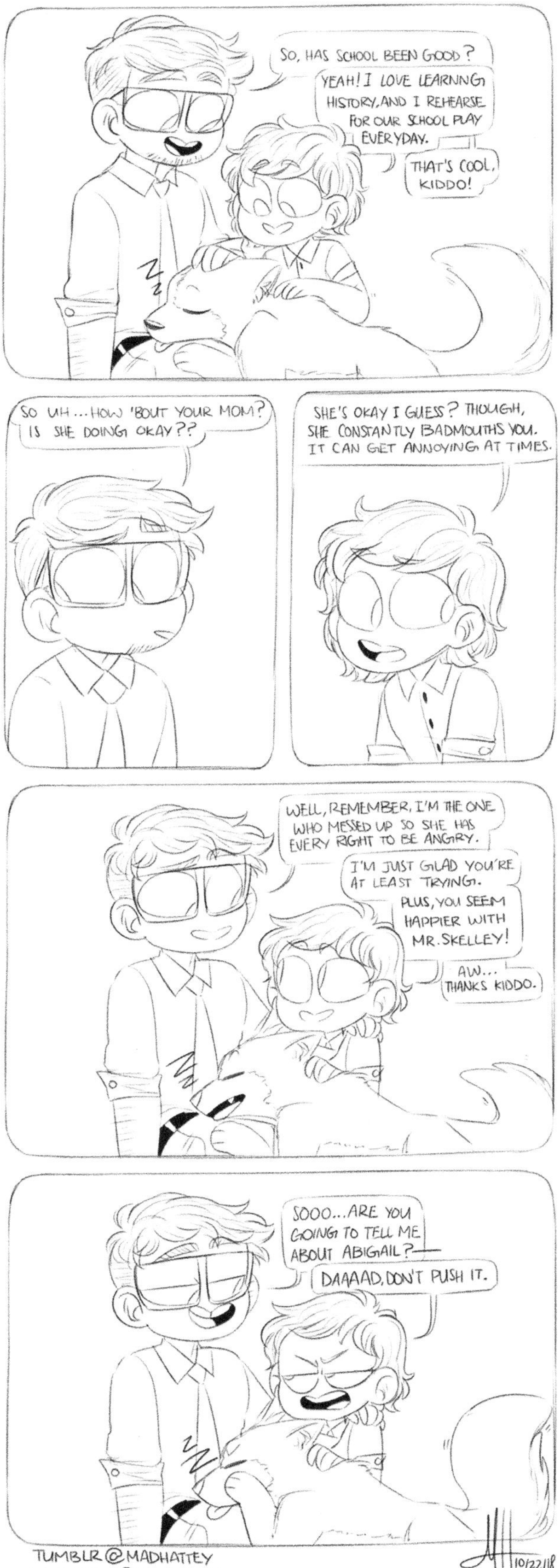

TUMBLR @MADHATTEY
INSTAGRAM @MADHATTEY

10/22/18

84

85

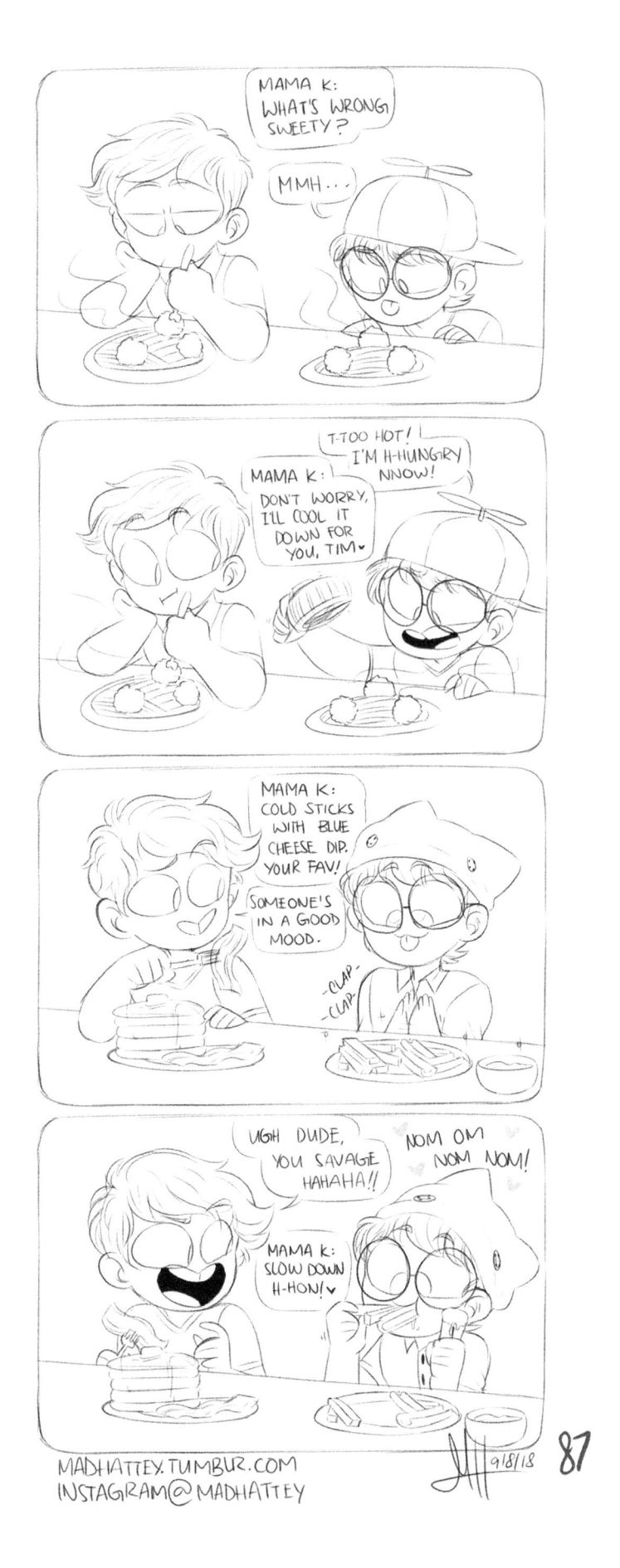

MADHATTEY.TUMBLR.COM
INSTAGRAM@MADHATTEY

MADHATTEY.TUMBLR.COM
INSTAGRAM @MADHATTEY

89

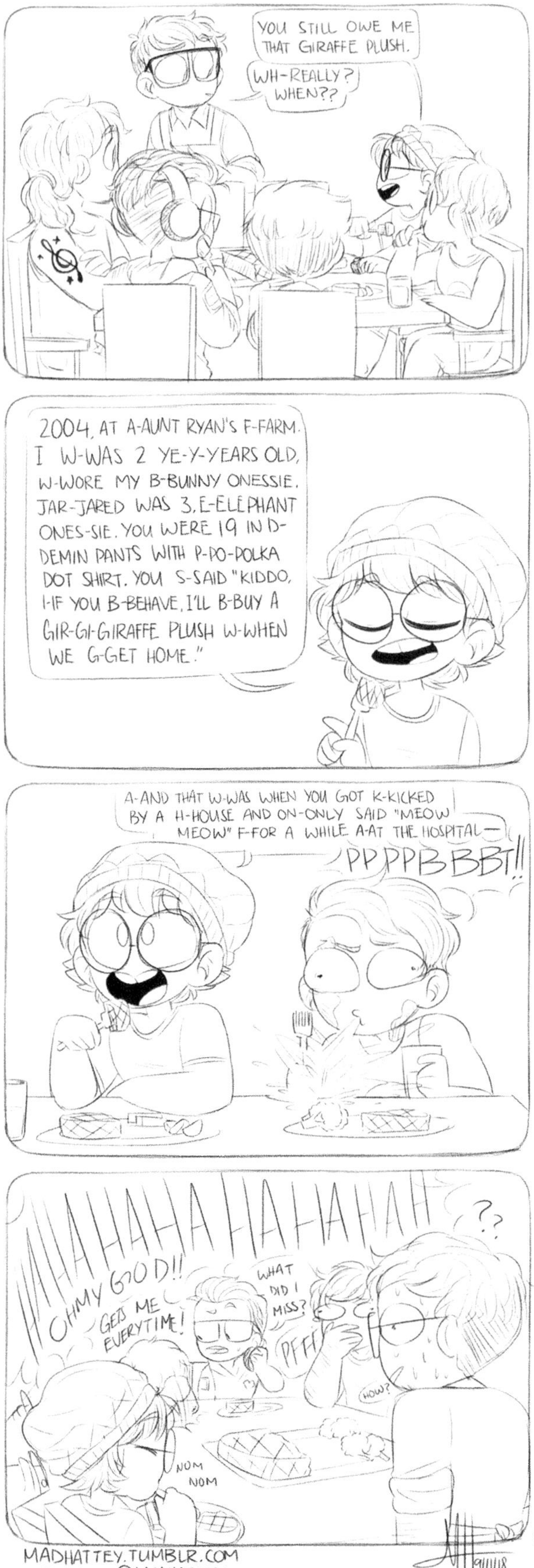

MADHATTEY.TUMBLR.COM
INSTAGRAM@MADHATTEY

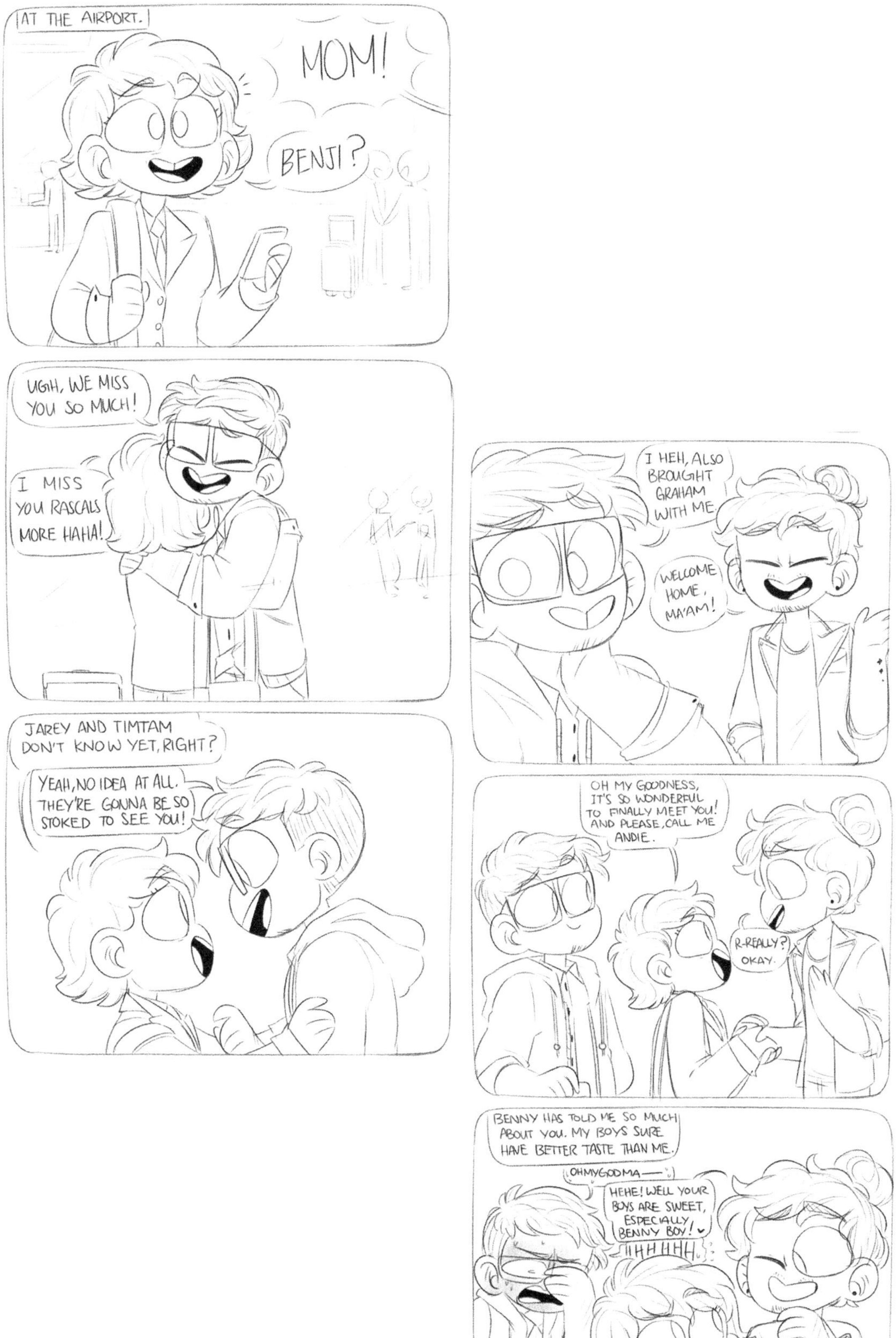

THEKLEINMANBROTHERS.WORDPRESS.COM

93

TIME TO BLOW THE CANDLES, TIMTAM!
HAPPY BIRTHDAY, BUDDY ♥
COOL CAKE.
YAYY!
CLAP
CLAP
CLAP
POP!!
AAAAAA
T-TIM, IT'S O-OKAY!
SHE DIDN'T MEAN IT, KIDDO.
WHAT THE HELL?!?
WAAAA
YOU NEED CONTROL YOUR KID, HE'S INSANE!
EXCUSE ME?? HE'S AUTISTIC!
WELL, HOW CONVENIENT—
THERE YOU GO! MR.BUNNINGTON IS ALWAYS HERE.
MMMH... HMM...
STOP TALKING ABOUT MY SON LIKE THAT!
YOU NEED TO LEAVE!
UGH. WHATEVER.

ALRIGHT SO, CHRISMUKKAH FEAST!
WHAT DO YOU GUYS WANNA EAT THIS YEAR?
EVERYTHING, BUT WAY. MORE. DONUTS!
J-JE-JELLY FILLINGS!!
NOT TOO MANY LIKE LAST YEAR.
YEAH, I SPOILED YOU BOYS TOO MUCH—
AW COME ON MA, WE WERE PERFECTLY FINE.
IT W-WASN'T THAT B-BAD!
LAST YEAR
I TOLD YOU BOYS TO TAKE IT EATHY.
B-BUT YOU M-MADE SO M-MA-MANY AND THEY T-TASTE SOOOO G-GO-GOOOOD..

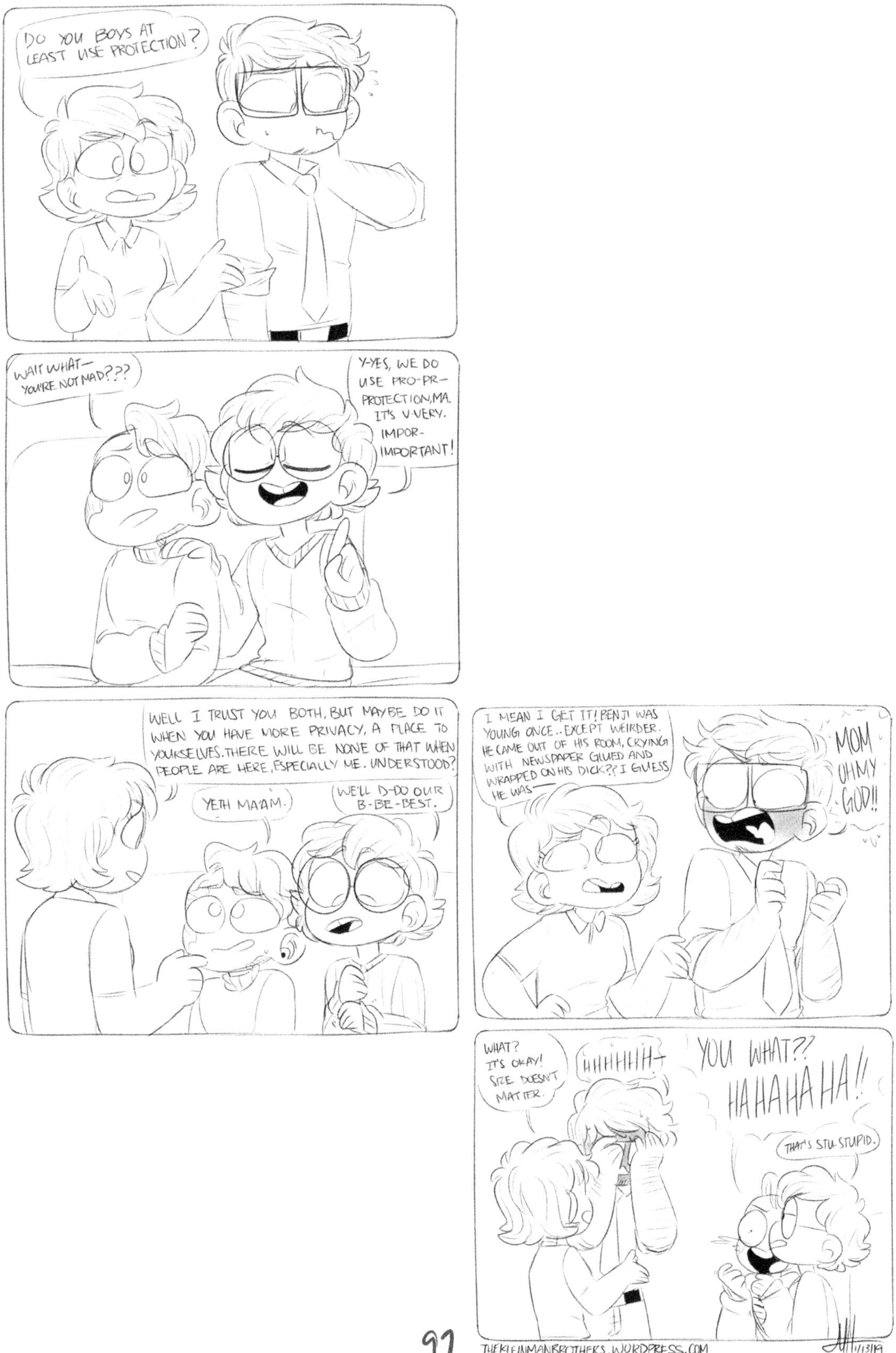

THEKLEINMANBROTHERS.WORDPRESS.COM

98

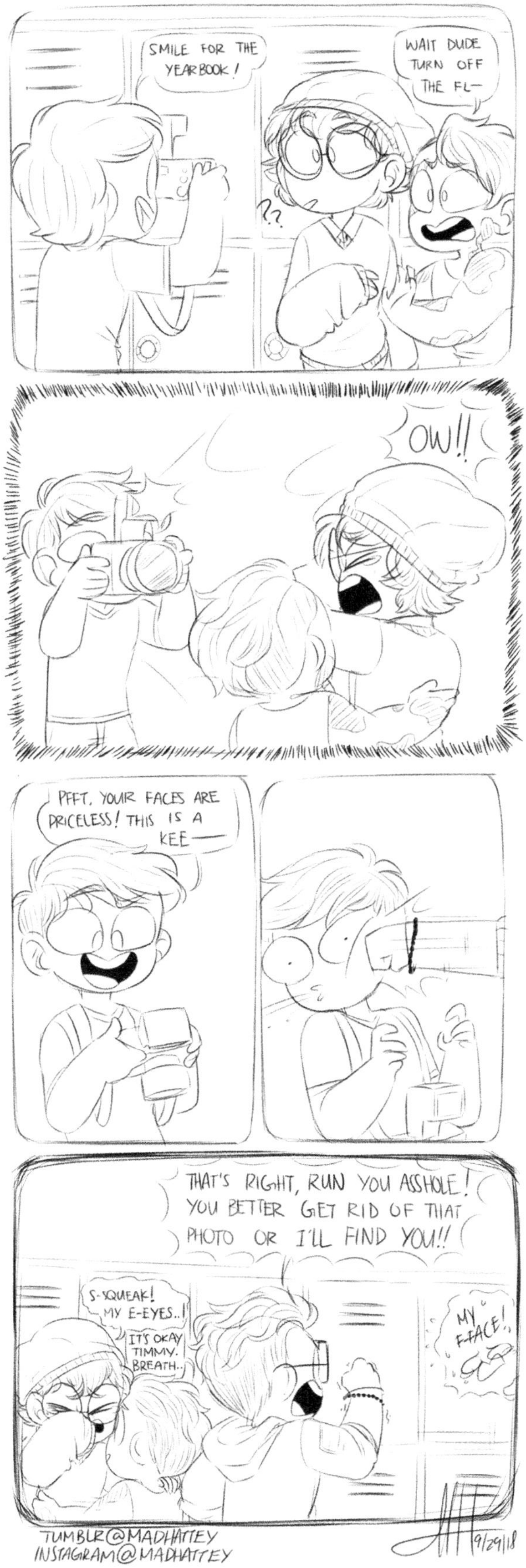

TUMBLR@MADHATTEY
INSTAGRAM@MADHATTEY

SOOOO, ARE YOU THAYING YOU FORGIVE ME——
I ONLY TRY TO LIKE YOU CAUSE TIMMY LOVES YOUR STUPID FACE. SO YOU BETTER WATCH YOURSELF.
HEH! FAIR ENOUGH.
ARE YOU JUST MAD THAT I MIGHT BEAT YOU AT SMASH AGAIN——
SHUT UP BEFORE I SHOVE A BLUE SHELL UP YOUR ASS.
PFFT! I'M JUST SAYING——
!!
HONEY, YOU'RE SO DRAMATIC, IT'S JUST AN ANNIVERSARY. I'LL CALL YOU BACK..
... HEY. YOU OKAY, DUDE?
I.. I THOUGHT I.. HEARD MY DAD...
IT WAS JUST ANOTHER GUY. YOUR FATHER CAN'T GET YOU.
BUT.. WHAT IF..?
EY, HE'S NOT GETTING ANYWHERE NEAR YOU. REMEMBER, TIMMY IS COOKING YOUR FAVORITE! AND WE'RE ALL PLAYING MARIO PARTY. ALRIGHT, RICH?
...YEAH.. OKAY..

101

102

UH... GRAY?
HM?
I'VE SAID I.. I LOVE YOU RIGHT? YOU'RE THE B-BEST PERSON I EVER MET.
HEH, YEAH YOU'VE SAID IT AN INIFINITE AMOUNT OF TIMES
ISN'T THAT B—?
DUDE, MIND YOUR OWN BUSINESS.
YOU SURE THIS IS OKAY, BENNY?
MHM! I'M HAPPY, HON. LET THEM STARE ~

WHAT IS DEAR EVAN HANSEN?

DEH tells the story of a young man with social anxiety disorder who so yearns to make a connection with his peers that he fabricates a relationship with a deceased student to become closer to the boy's family. When a student commits suicide, shy Evan Hansen finds himself at the center of tragedy and turmoil. In a misguided attempt to comfort the boy's grieving family, Evan pretends that he was good friends with their son. He invents a fabricated email account to "prove" their friendship, and when a fake suicide note makes its way online, Evan finds himself the unintended face of a viral video about loneliness and friendship.

WHAT IS BE MORE CHILL?

"More than survive." That's all Jeremy Heere wants out of high school. But looking up from the bottom of the social ladder, there's little hope for the uncool Jeremy. What if there was an easy way to change all that? Enter the SQUIP, a Japanese nanocomputer in the form of an easy-to-swallow pill. The SQUIP will implant itself in your brain and tell you what to wear, what to say, and how to act to achieve ultimate coolness. Seems like an easy choice, right? But when the SQUIP takes an unexpected, darker turn, is Jeremy willing to lose his best friend, his crush, his classmates, and the whole world, all in effort to be more chill? Set to a hot-pop rock score by Joe Iconis, Be More Chill is a hilarious sci-fi tale of high school and one boy's quest to fit in.

THE BABIES

Timmy — Is me — Savage Cheese Enthusiast

Dustin — My BFF ♥ — good I guess — Best boy!

Jared — Best Annoying Bro — Stinky! — please stop farting.

Reva — badass lawyer & MOM — most beautiful

Benji — bear MOM — Chonky

Martin — best Dad. — Hero!

Evan — tree boy — Shy Acorn.

Rich — loud stinky rooster — Pretty — Sexy Bae — Handsome Rooster

Dani — everybody's sunshine — Best itty bitty bby

106

THEORIZE THE STORY:

COMING SOON..
JARED'S STORY.

FEEL FREE TO COLOR THE COMIC AND THIS SKETCH!

JAKE DILLINGER
©BMC-MARGIE

* THIS IS MARGIE'S VERSION OF JAKE.

Bleh
©BMC-DEH MAR2SIE
☆ THESE ARE HATTEY & MAR2SIES' VERSIONS OF THEM.

HONORABLE MENTIONS:

KELLY WIFEY ♥ (WE WRITE THE STORY OF RICH AND TIMMY.)

BRUH MARZSIE ♥ (DUSTIN/MADELINE ENTHUSIAST AND MY CO-WRITER!)

BRO ALEX ♥ (SWEET FILTHY BOY + GOOD WRITER)

ABRAHAM ♥ (LONG LOST SON)

MY CHILDHOOD FRIENDOS

STEFANIE (MUSIC + WRITING BBY)

JUSTIN ♥ (SMART FOUR-EYES)

OLD INTERNET FRIENDOS

ROXY FOXY ♥ (GAMING BBY)

DELI ♥ (CREATIVE BBY)

MOMMY MAE ♥ (REBEL/CRITIC/WONDER WOMAN)

SISTER ARIELLE ♥ (LITTLE MERMAID/BTS SUPER FAN)

KUYA BENJI ♥ (BALUGA BOY + FUNNY BUTT)

LOLA VIGIE ♥ (BEST GRANDMA)

ATE ZINNIA ♥ (BEST SMOL AUNT)

TRIBBI ♥ (SPOILED SWEET BOY)

LOLO RUBEN ♥ (BEST MUSIC DAD)

THANK YOU FOR INSPIRING ME TO BE THE PERSON I AM TODAY. ILY ♥

THANKS FOR READING MY MADNESS!

FIND ME HERE:
- MADHATTEY.COM
- INSTAGRAM.COM/MADHATTEY
- TWITTER.COM/HATTEYMCGARBAGE
- MADHATTEY @ YOUTUBE
- MADHATTEY @ REDBUBBLE ← MY STORE!

ALSO CHECK OUT:
- THEKLEINMANBROTHERS.WORDPRESS.COM
  [BE MORE SINCERE MUSICAL CROSSOVER]
- BEMORECHILLMUSICAL.COM
- DEAREVANHANSEN.COM

FIND THEM HERE:
- INSTAGRAM.COM/MARZSIE
- INSTAGRAM.COM/CASPERARTS

Made in the USA
Las Vegas, NV
27 February 2021